DESIRING DEATH

by

C. P. MANDARA

Chimera (*ki-mir'a, ki-*)
a creation of the imagination, a wild fantasy...

www.chimerabooks.co.uk

ISBN 9781780804347

New authors are always welcome, or if you're already a published author and have existing work, the rights of which remain with or have reverted to you, we would love to hear from you at **info@chimerabooks.co.uk**.

Desiring Death published in 2015 by Chimera Books.

Cover design by Kriss Morton of Cabin Goddess Graphics.

This novel is fiction - in real life practice safe sex.

Contents

A thousand times we die in one life. We crumble, break and tear apart until the layers of illusion are burned away and all that is left, is the truth of who and what we really are. *Teal Scott*

Running

Her lungs were burning. There was a tight knot in her chest that threatened to explode given half a chance, and four limbs that were fuelled by nothing more than lactic acid. The sandy grit underneath her bare feet ripped them to shreds, but she was beyond caring. All that mattered was distance. She had been given the chance to run and she intended to make full use of it. He would pursue her, of that she had no doubt.

Breathe, just breathe, she implored her lungs. A ragged sound tore through her and the substance she finally managed to suck into her body was too little, too late. Her level of adrenaline was beginning to wane and the breakneck pace she had set for herself would not be maintained for long. Another tortured breath was forced into her chest as she kept her feet moving one in front of the other.

Concentrating on her surroundings she willed herself to think of nothing more than the slippery cobblestones beneath her feet. He could read every thought in her head and by that alone he would track her. Don't think... don't think, she pleaded with herself, but as her level of panic increased her concentration began to falter. Staring at the obsidian water of the canal below, feeling her feet slide on the slick carpet of stones beneath her as she stumbled forwards, she screamed. Soft, male laughter echoed inside her head. She stumbled again and searing pain shot through her fractured shoulder, nearly crippling her with its intensity.

'Run and hide my precious little pet, but rest assured you'll be in my bed before this night is out.'

Violetta gasped and a strangled sob escaped her throat.

'Don't you find it highly amusing that the huntress has now become the hunted?' The voice taunted her, but she knew better than to respond. With her legs buckling underneath her she ran as fast as she could towards St Mark's Basilica. She needed to be inside holy walls if there was to be any hope of winning this battle.

A lone gondola made her jump as it sliced through the black water, its oars making tiny splashes at regular intervals. Looking over in its direction frantically, wondering if her tormentor would be behind the iron prow-head, she couldn't help but breathe a sigh of relief as a handsome young Italian proffered his straw hat in her direction, touting for business. She didn't give him a further glance as she continued on towards her destination.

'Wherever you're headed, I will find you, Violetta. You can run, but hiding is out of the question. I am inside your mind. I can read your every thought as it begins to grow inside your head. You are mine and I intend to have my revenge. You will pay in every way imaginable. I'm going to rip that proud and self-assured demeanour of yours apart and rebuild you, from the bottom up. You'll hang off my every word, you'll beg to service me in my bed *and* out of it, and most importantly, you'll live solely to please me. Until I choose to kill you, of course. Does that sound like a fitting revenge, Violetta? After all those deaths you have viciously doled out to my family, wouldn't you like to atone to your maker in some way?'

'You are a monster! I have no need to atone for anything.' The words tumbled out of her frothing mouth in a barely legible, garbled stream, but he would have heard them. He heard everything. Realising her error, her feet desperately tried to pick up their pace, but they had little left to give. Her heartbeat was banging a hole in her chest and air had become a precious commodity that was about as abundant as gold dust. She knew with a fatalistic certainty that she would never make it to the cathedral. Her body would give out long before St. Mark's square came into view. She wanted to sob hysterically, but the little energy she had left needed to be preserved. There must be some way out of this mess. There had to be.

Looking up at the long row of three story apartment buildings that lined the canal, she saw that even though the time was well past midnight Venice was disinclined to sleep. The soft glow of ochre light that spilled from worn, wooden shutters should have enchanted and mesmerised her. The ornate stone framework that encircled both windows and doors ought to have been a delight to behold, as were the beautiful, cheerful colours of the paintwork in hues of tangerine, lemon and terracotta, but nothing served to bring a smile to her face. Violetta's world was crumbling around her and once it splintered there would be no repairing it. Time was not on her side.

A soft chuckle chose that moment to reverberate around her head. He was playing with her. It was a game of cat and mouse, and she was the smaller animal of the two. Damn it! She had just broadcast her position with a neon flag. What a stupidly foolish thing to do. Her brain was obviously dissolving into mush. *Oh God, oh God, oh God*. Panic began to overwhelm her. She had no claws that could compete with his. No one would run to her aid. She was supposed to have been the best of the best, or had been until this evening's debacle. Her feet picked up their pace once again as his laughter abruptly ended. Her head darted about over her shoulders, trying to catch a glimpse of him, but there was little chance she would see him unless he wanted to be seen. The beast would remain hidden, a mere figment of her imagination, until she had expended every last drop of energy she possessed. Then her fate would be decided, unless she determined to carve herself a new one and the options, to her mind, were somewhat limited and ultimately fatal.

When Violetta had been contracted to kill Martinet she had expected it to be business as usual. This was not arrogance on her part, as she was exceptionally talented at her profession. Doling out death with skill and exacting precision, many a vampire had tumbled to their demise from her quick hands and lightning-fast reflexes. For the last few years, it had hardly been much of a challenge and she had found herself thinking of ways to make the chase more entertaining. How foolish did that make her feel now? This evening she had become sloppy. She had not completed her homework. As a result of that, she would be lucky to survive more than a few days. If Martinet captured her, and the odds were decidedly stacked on his side, then he would probably tire of her quickly. If he didn't get bored and snap her neck in two, he would drain her dry. Human victims didn't usually live much past the denominator of a week.

Her thoughts fled back to the masked ball earlier and the run up of events which had led to this mess. He'd been waiting for her outside the gardens of the Castello Verde. She'd approached him cautiously enough, but hadn't taken any great pains to observe or scrutinize his behaviour. That was her first mistake. If she had taken the trouble to examine the waxen tint of his skin or the incredible cobalt blue of his irises, she might have at least thought to ask for back-up. Her second mistake had been in underestimating his age. He'd been turned somewhere around his mid-thirties and the long, dark hair that curled enticingly at his neck had given him a youthful air of one younger than that, but you estimated a vampire's real age by the translucency of their skin. When she'd had the chance to get a glimpse of him up close he'd had barely a wrinkle upon him. He was flawless perfection all over and that did not bode well. That signified he had been alive for at least a century, maybe more, and it meant he would prove very difficult to kill.

As the father of the children she had slain it was expected that he would be the hardest to destroy, but she had never dreamt it would be virtually impossible. When he had set his sights upon her, flaring his hypnotic blue eyes to their widest potential, an intense pulse of fear had circulated around her body, one that had not crossed her features in several years.

'You have the gift,' she had whispered. Her emotions were tumbling around inside her body. Dread, shock, horror and the need to run as fast and as far as her legs would carry her. Although she had never actually met a vampire who carried 'the gift', she had heard about it. Tales of vivid, neon eyes that could rip through a person's mind and take away every secret they possessed had been used to scare her when she was nothing more than a fledgling. She had thought them flights of fancy, having never seen evidence to the contrary, but now she knew differently. The gift was painfully real and it was more manipulating than even she could have believed. He could control her every movement, the use of her voice, slow or speed up her heartbeat, and even induce desire by deploying her own hormones. How humiliating that had been; wrapped in his arms in the great throng of the Castello's ballroom, being spun around the dancing lights of the beautiful Italian chandeliers, and staring up at him with fluttering lashes and doe eyes. Urgh.

There was another chuckle inside her head. This time she did not even pause as her footfalls continued to splatter a pathway towards their goal. She'd let him enjoy these humble thoughts. At least they would prevent him from gaining any further information on her whereabouts. He'd probably pinpointed her position fairly accurately from her earlier clues, but all she could do now was employ damage control. How did you compete with an adversary who could read your mind? As the thought entered her head she banished it and dived down a dark narrow alleyway, careful to keep her feet moving forward and her mind on the past.

Martinet had allowed her a chance at killing him. Now it seemed incredible, even to her. Did he want to die? Or had he already known he was invincible? Most vampires did not go quietly to their graves; quite the opposite in fact. They usually fought with the most amazing tenacity. What was his deal? It was exasperating, but after having tried her hardest to kill him using every trick in the book, he appeared unbreakable. Wooden stakes had simply bounced off him and her solid silver blade hadn't made a mark on the pristine skin of his neck. He was the first vampire to have dulled her blade, and she was still reeling from the shock. It appeared she had just picked a fight with the most dangerous vampire in the land, and what was more, he intended to make her pay for the blunder with her life.

Whilst he had given her an opportunity to kill him without his interference, there had been conditions attached to his offer. Quite sizable and serious conditions, to her mind:

'If you fail, I fancy you'll be the first of my new breed of children. Depending on how exacting my desire for revenge is, I might even take you for a bride, an eternal one, Violetta.'

At the time she had felt confident of her success. Without his glowing blue eyes upon her, she felt she stood more than a fighting chance of ending his miserable existence. How wrong had she been? His words echoed in her head once more. No, not that, never that, please help her, God. It would be a fate worse than death. Death could be quick and painless or it could be a long, drawn out and painful affair, but it would never be as bad as the reincarnation of her body as a vampire, enslaved to *him.*

When he had initially issued his threat she thought he required a blood-slave or a servant to cook and clean for him. He had quickly disabused her of that notion. He wanted a warm, willing body underneath his and he intended to do terrible things with her. The man wanted to play with her and he wanted sex! No one had ever been allowed near her body. A huntress was supposed to keep herself pure and untouched. Killing vampires was almost a religion in itself and she was told she needed no further complications that relationships with the male gender would inevitably provide. Besides, a watchful eye was kept upon her at all times. At the slightest fraternisation with a man her mentor would frown at her, shake her head, and Violetta would meekly obey orders and stand behind the ranks of her peers. She had known the sacrifices the job would entail. She hadn't realised how onerous they would be as each year passed, but she could hardly cry foul now.

Diverting her attention back, to concentrate on the events of the evening and not the scenery around her, she was careful to make sure that her eyes focused on little more than the uneven sea of worn cobblestones beneath her feet. She would not give him any further clues to her whereabouts. She couldn't afford to give him anything, for the tiniest mistake on her behalf could result in an expiry date on her life that was about sixty years sooner than she'd hoped for.

Her thoughts turned to dwell on her last attempt at extinguishing his life, back in the Castello's gardens. She'd hit the ground with such force that something inside her snapped and it hadn't been her temper, unfortunately. Excruciating pain radiated down from her left shoulder on contact with the hard earth and it brought tears to her eyes. It was unlike anything she had ever known, and at first it had been an effort just to force simple words from her mouth. When he had insisted they go back to the crowded ballroom and dance, she looked at him in horror and issued her refusal.

'You will do anything I tell you to, and believe me when I say that your pain will be my pleasure.'

What those words had done to her body! Reliving them now caused a sharp shudder of longing to rip through her and she was chagrined to find that the arousal she felt was all very much her own. Martinet was too attractive, too perfect, too arrogant for his own good, and... her libido seemed to respond to that in the oddest way. Hot floods of heat washed through her cheeks and the warmth worked its way downwards, finding an epicentre at the juncture of her thighs. For the first time in her life her panties had become wet. Not just a little bit damp, but absolutely sodden. It had been a humiliating experience, made one hundred times worse by the fact that he could read her mind. She could almost feel him rooting around in her brain, wondering what little titbit he could use to best advantage later. How did you compete with someone like that? How did you fight back? Every time he asked her a question the answer nearly burst its way past her lips in its eagerness to escape. It was clear that humans were nothing more than puppets to him; worthless beings that could be played with and manipulated to dance to his every tune. She would be his new toy and it would give him great pleasure to break her, if she allowed herself to be caught. She almost laughed to herself at the thought. Who was she kidding? It was hardly like she had a choice in the matter.

She remembered the bright lights of the ballroom and the dazzle and glare as her eyes had adjusted from the darkness of the garden, her head automatically positioning itself in the hard curve of his neck. It galled her no end to realise Martinet could control her with such ease. If he'd let her go she would have fallen to her knees in agony. Her arm was in a state of furious pain which demanded all of her attention. Being spun around in a dizzying arc of flowing organza and curling ribbons only served to compound the throbbing bone and she had desperately wanted to beg for his mercy. Her pride had kept her from uttering the feeble words, but only just. It didn't much matter. The beast knew everything that went on in her head. He had offered to take 'the nasty ache away', his words not hers, but there had been a catch to his benevolent gesture.

'Your complete surrender, my dear. Your capitulation to my every whim and desire. Oh, and your soul, of course.'

She'd declined his touching offer, but Martinet wasn't the type to take no for an answer. He'd retaliated by thrusting himself into her mind and propelling her into a stone cavern, his bedroom, if she wasn't much mistaken. He'd then laid his filthy hands all over her and damned if she hadn't enjoyed it. His touch kindled fires that she hadn't known existed and now she'd been introduced to the sensation she wanted more, but not from him. Violetta recalled the beautifully carved, dark oak posts of his four-poster bed, the crimson drapes and the matching satin sheets. It was a well-cared for antiquity that would easily have had several noughts attached to its price tag. Breathtakingly beautiful, the sight of it, when she had dared to look a little closer, made her shudder. The vision of shiny steel handcuffs and reels of black, hessian rope that adorned the posts would be forever burned into her mind. How many other humans, she wondered, had he toyed with in this way? Or was it possible she would be the first? It seemed doubtful. He'd probably had lots of practice at corrupting innocent young minds and polluting their flesh. At that thought more laughter appeared and echoed inside her head, bouncing around madly like a team of toddlers at a birthday party. How dare he invade her mind!

'Oh, you have no idea how much I would dare to do, both to that exquisitely beautiful body of yours and to your mind. I will enjoy every single second of my revenge, chérie. I will play your body like Mozart played the piano, but better and with more enthusiasm. My hands, my lips and my tongue will bring you to life and they will teach you things you've never even dreamt off. It will be the sweetest pleasure and the most terrible torment to endure my training, Violetta.'

Trying desperately hard to shut his voice out of her head, she concentrated on reaching her destination. Her run had now slowed to a pathetically brisk walk, but she ploughed on as fast and as hard as she was able. Gritting her teeth against the fierce pain that emanated from her shoulder, she knew it wouldn't be long before the Piazza San Marco came into view.

'I will teach you to worship my touch. You will learn that your place is beside me, kneeling at my feet.'

She snorted with laughter, even though it cost her dearly, for the throb of her shoulder brought tears to her eyes. Cradling the injured limb in her free arm she stumbled forward and tried to ignore his insistent presence.

'You will be trained in the arts of pleasure, obedience and servitude. You will excel at them all, and when I get bored of tasting the delicious vintage that flows throughout your body I will change you and then your torment will really begin. Will you fight me, Violetta?'

She couldn't help herself and riposted back with, 'Every step of the damn way.'

'Good,' was his succinct reply, followed by, 'how's the neck?'

Violetta gave a strangled wail. She had wanted to forget their last little foray back at the Castello. He had uttered demands that she send her colleagues packing, of which she immediately refused. They were the only safety net she had left after he'd revealed his many considerable and unsavoury talents. Martinet was clever, though, and knew he'd have to get rid of them if he stood a reasonable chance at abducting her. Alas, it had taken him no more than a few seconds to achieve his goal. Another thrust and he'd anchored himself in her head once more, but this time he was taking no prisoners.

'Tsk, tsk. This simply won't do. You've yet to learn the consequences of disobeying me, but you will, chérie. When I say jump you say how high, how far, and in what direction?'

With those ominous words her head had exploded in a gruesome blood bath.

Martinet visually demonstrated exactly what he would do to her friends if she chose to disobey him, and it wasn't in the least bit pretty. He'd inserted himself inside her brain while he ripped heads from necks, tore through flesh and bone with his talons, and his finale, to really hammer his point home, had been his fist tearing a beating heart out through her mother's chest. Her mind had nearly crumbled to ashes. She'd pleaded with him to stop his vision and begged to be set free of its malice. He'd let her go, but on the condition that she get rid of her accomplices.

'Tell your friends that you are about to finish me off in the gardens and will return with the evidence in due course. That is what they usually expect, is it not?'

She had replied, somewhat shakily, with the news that they would require blood for evidence of his death. It would be a little tricky to provide if he intended to live through the experience. Vampires did not relinquish their precious red nectar easily. The reasons were many, but the most important was that they surrendered power and strength with each drop lost. To the undead, a drop of the red stuff was their most precious belonging.

'They will get it: yours, but don't worry, your wound will not be mortal. Now be a good girl and get over there before I renege on our deal and begin a storm of carnage that would impress Genghis Khan.'

She had not doubted for a moment that his threat was real. The look in his eyes as he said it had been unholy, to say the least.

Having no option but to appear to obey his words she watched him stalk off to the gardens once more, now awaiting her presence as the almighty huntress. Violetta had been nearly paralysed with fear for a moment, which was laughable. The huntress had become the hunted. She'd been backed into a very small corner where someone's hands remained constantly around her throat, waiting for the slightest provocation to tighten them. She could not think out a plan of attack. He was inside her mind and body, an insidious presence that would watch over every move she made. He had the power to force words from her lips, make her run, dance, hop or jig merrily to whatever tune he chose to play. He could also, humiliatingly, control all her bodily functions. She was at his utter mercy, and he did not appear to be in the least bit merciful with regards to her life. He wanted to play with her and torment her, as a cat would plague an injured bird: to the death, and more frighteningly, perhaps beyond.

What he didn't know, though, was that her little brain was a lot smarter than it appeared. She hadn't lost all of her cards - not yet. There were some things that you always kept close to your chest.

Watering the Garden

Martinet had stopped the pain radiating out from her shoulder as she made a beeline towards the gathered crowd of her friends, but she didn't think him any less of a monster for his small kindness. If he'd wanted her to speak in a calm, even voice, and be in the slightest bit believable, it was the very least he'd have to do. The speed in which he'd managed to set her body to rights had been astounding though. One minute she'd been crippled with agony, heart racing, skin deathly white and barely able to get a word past her dry lips. In the next her cheeks were once again rosy in colour, eyes sparkling with health and her breathing returned to a slow and easy pace. Violetta was gliding across the parquet floor of the ballroom as if she hadn't a care in the world, a hand flouncing up to caress a lock of red hair as she toyed with it in a flirtatious manner. He prevented the growl that wanted to escape from her throat at his meddling interference.

'I am not trying to attract a suitor, so leave me be.' She pushed the thought at him with a little more force than necessary and knew he'd received it when she heard his answering laugh.

'Bored of suitors already, Violetta? How many have you had in that short lifespan of yours? Can't be more than a couple, can it?'

The reply of 'none' wanted to fly from her lips, but she managed to hold it in, barely, while she directed her thoughts towards puncturing his body with numerous sharp and delightfully pointed instruments of death.

'My, my, my, such temper in one so young. You'll need to learn to control that, sweetness, or I assure you there'll be repercussions.' It was clear by the tone of his voice that Martinet was amused and, if anything, it just infuriated her more.

'I will never stop trying to kill you,' she bit back telepathically. 'Every waking moment you will need to watch me, because if you let down your guard for the merest instance and I find a way of ending you, it will be done. Leave me here, beast, and go find one of your own kind to torment.'

'Oh, I would,' came the soft and menacing reply, 'but you've killed all the ones in these parts, I believe.' The voice that uttered those words was deadly.

A flash of horrific pain hit her as he let her shoulder make its presence known once more. There was a tight gasp and her feet went out from under her, pitching her body forward into the thronging crowds. Almost as soon as it had appeared, the pain vanished - but it had served its purpose as a warning. Violetta would have to guard her viperish tongue or face the consequences. Setting out both arms to steady herself she apologised to the portly gentleman she had just careened into, and exchanged the required pleasantries before making her excuses to depart. The balding man, whose eyes had taken on a luminous gleam at having such a pretty maiden fall at his feet, held on to her arm for a few seconds longer than necessary. With a little effort on her part she managed to wrench herself away with a smile and continue forward to her objective. What would she say to them? Was it possible they would believe her lies? Eleanor, an older huntress and her mentor, would see through her in a second. She would have to direct her speech at someone less astute. Connaught was the obvious choice. He was still a good friend but not on the same personal level as her so-called 'mother'. He would not be able to read her so keenly. He would not smell the lie. At least, she hoped he wouldn't, for the lives of her friends rested upon him believing her. She had no doubt that Martinet would carry through with his threats if she failed and create a massacre of the grandest proportions. Better one life to be hers, than all of her comrades.

'So noble, Violetta,' he drawled in a bored fashion. 'Do get on with it, dear, or I may have to get out my hankie.'

Her back wanted to stiffen at his comment and her tongue wanted to lash out, but neither options were apparently available to her, so it was with great chagrin that she found herself smiling sweetly and turning her face around to address Connaught with his familiar nickname.

'Con, I've found him,' she whispered, in a sickly sweet girly voice that was full of excitement and awe. They were not her own words and the inflection upon them was all Martinet's own. He manipulated her with far too much skill and for that alone she wanted to scratch his eyes out. In her head she was horrified that he'd already began plucking secrets from her mind, and what was even more galling was the knowledge that it would be the first of many. He had her at his complete and utter mercy.

'Good girl,' whispered Con, with a congratulatory wink and a pat on the back. It was clear that he suspected nothing was amiss by his relaxed posture and wide smile. 'Now that you have him where you want him, what are you going to do with him?' The question was an old one and said for rhetorical effect, but she didn't feel the desire to smile as she normally would have. Alas, Martinet had other plans for her. Tinkling peals of laughter erupted from her throat and her face returned Con's large grin.

'Be back in five minutes,' she cooed, while her hands flounced the folds of her dress back and forth. She wanted to roll her eyes at the ridiculously childish action, but that, too, was denied her.

'Sort him out, Vi, and make it snappy. You know how Eleanor hates these stuffy affairs. She's been looking at her watch for the past half hour and snapping everybody's head off.'

Violetta knew the feeling. Wanting to grind her teeth painfully together, instead she formed a bright smile of farewell and gave Con a little wave as her feet began to move once again. Her hands itched to run themselves through Con's fine, sandy hair as she often did in a manner of friendly affection, but she had no control of them tonight. Walking off into the distance, towards the soulless black of midnight, it felt bizarre to realise that she wasn't in the least bit afraid. Even her emotions were under his command. It was a sombre, if not somewhat dismal thought. Did she have a hope in hell of getting out of this mess? Positive thinking, she berated herself. Where there was a will... there had better be a way, because she was far too young to die.

The sounds of chatter faded away slowly as her feet searched for a secure landing place on the soft grass. The beautifully groomed gardens were the reason the Green Castle, or Castello Verde, had acquired its name. In the daylight they were truly stunning and home to all manner of flora and fauna. At night twinkling solar lights keep the pathways alive but the vibrant colours of the flowers were snuffed out. Petals hid, stamens cowered in their protective green casings and everything took on shades of grey and black. It could pretty much be the state of her own continued wretched existence, if Martinet were to be believed. Speaking of the vamp, where on earth was the guy? As her eyes scanned left and right there was not even the merest flicker of movement that could be detected in the humid night air. There was barely a breeze, very little noise, and it left her feeling eerily... alone. Spinning around in a three hundred and sixty degree circle she confirmed what she already knew. The place was deserted. Maybe he had decided to let her go after all? Maybe the beast had the tiniest twinge of conscience and... her thoughts broke off abruptly as a figure flew from the rooftops and landed behind her. Before she had recovered from the shock an arm flew round her neck in a tight arc and began constricting her airway.

'Drop that pretty little glass vial you've got hidden away in your right hand, now.'

That the voice and arm belonged to Martinet was not in question. He injected the words into her ear with such rancour that she wondered if he'd kill her there and then. A few seconds of terrorised silence passed. His grip tightened around her throat. Gurgling in protest, her hand stubbornly clutched the precious little bottle even more tightly, because it might be the only lifeline she had left.

'You're a tenacious little chit, aren't you?' He growled as he shook her body forcibly. 'Do you really want me to employ "other" tactics?'

She burbled insensibly as he began to cut off her air supply, but she didn't drop her precious cargo. If he was going to kill her, then it would be better if it were sooner rather than later.

'You surprise me, Miss...' He let the sentence hang in mid-air and Violetta felt him give her a push to answer it. She held on to the words that threatened to erupt from her lips, even though it was a hard won battle.

He frowned. 'I'll stamp that wilfulness out of your body, Violetta. Mark my words. All you are doing is waving a bright red banner in front of my face saying "spank me", and the outcome for your arse, delectable though it may be, isn't looking good.' Sarcasm dripped off his tongue.

While Violetta did not respond to his words she did stop struggling. The intelligent part of her brain said that the action was worthless, for his strength more than quadrupled hers. Feeling her hands shake around the smooth glass vial and a bead of sweat drip down her neck, she wondered why he didn't just pluck the offending item from her fingers and smash it against the wall. He was more than capable of such a feat.

'Ah, but where would be the fun in that? It's much more amusing to watch you do my dirty work for me, and the more painful and unpalatable you find my ideas, the better.' His arm softened around her throat, but she did not feel in the slightest bit relieved. 'Last chance, Vi. Drop the bottle.' Her spine stiffened at the use of her nickname, which had previously been reserved for friends, but her backbone did not waver. She would not drop her little present. He would have to take it from her. Smiling darkly at the thought, she imagined throwing the contents of the tiny tube all over his body and watching as his skin blistered and burned.

'Oh, I think not, precious,' he purred into her ear, and with his free hand he ran his fingers through the tempting, glossy red waves of her hair. Without warning his fist closed around a handful of her locks and yanked tightly downwards. Her head flew back sharply and her eyes immediately connected with two bright blue orbs that had danger written all over them.

'Your face looks so much better when it's immersed in pain. Not quite so smug now, are we?' His breath tickled her ear as his hand purchased an even tighter grip on her hair. The roots in her scalp began protesting at the cruel treatment. 'Drop it. Now.'

Violetta's head stung furiously as he forcibly tried to wrench several follicles out at once, but still she retained her tight grip on the bottle. 'What's to stop me from flicking the cork stopper out of this bottle and throwing the contents all over you?' She asked the question in a saccharine-sweet voice, laced with irony. They both knew he would not take the bottle from her. It was far too risky.

Sighing, Martinet released her hair and the impressive grip he had maintained around her neck, before walking backwards a couple of steps. She waited for something to happen, but the whole world had gone silent and the only thing she could hear was the sound of her strained breathing and a heartbeat that felt like it had just witnessed a murder. On the plus side, she guessed he had released his hold on her. Turning around slowly, she watched his steely gaze bearing down upon her. Her internal organs began to liquefy.

'Afraid, Violetta? What's stopping you?' He took another casual step back and lifted his arms in the air, as if urging her to do her worst. If that was the way he wanted to play things, so be it. Her thumb flicked at the cork stopper that held the precious water inside. Whilst there was probably only twenty centilitres of water held inside the small tube's confines, it would be enough. With a little hiss the cork popped free and there she was, holding her escape ticket, just a few scant inches away from her prey. All she needed to do was throw it. A quick flick of the wrist and her nightmare of an evening would be over. She would watch him writhe and roll around the floor in the throes of agony and not feel the slightest bit of remorse knowing she had delivered his last steps upon the planet earth. He was a monster that needed to be stopped. She was a trained huntress. She had been primed for this moment for the last ten years of her life. It was time to put that training to good use. She thrust the contents of the vial at him.

The Duchess

It would have been more accurate to say she tried to thrust the contents of the vial at him. Her brain sent down the order to her arm as requested, but her body did not compute the signal or perform the action required. Martinet had her fingers fixed in place and she couldn't move a single one of them.

'Scared?' Her eyes narrowed, and whilst she knew it was foolish to taunt him, she couldn't resist the impulse.

'Do I look scared?' He raised his eyebrows and glowering contempt descended upon her. The look he wore left her breathless with anticipation. Anticipation of what, she had no idea... but her body was certainly looking for something.

As his lips formed a wry smile she cursed herself for not trying to cover her thoughts. It was little wonder Martinet did not have a bride, for he would have been an insufferable husband to live with. A snort of laughter confirmed he'd heard her comment.

'Oh, you think so?' He smirked at her and unleashed the full power of his eyes upon her. She felt her blood go cold, ice literally flowing through her veins, as he locked down her body. The control he could wield with his mind was terrifying in the extreme. Even her vocal chords had been paralysed and try as she might, not a whisper could escape her lips.

'No, precious, you can stand there and listen to me for a moment,' he said. 'You're going to have to get used to listening to me, so we'll start practising now. You only get to speak when I ask you a direct question. That's rule number one. There will be many more, if you don't prove too tiresome, but that will do for the time being.' He moved forward slowly and caressed her cheek with one of his long, elegant fingers. 'Insufferable, you think?' He bit his lip and laughed merrily. 'That's not something I remember ever having been called before; stubborn, demanding and boorish, perhaps, but never insufferable. Most women would happily form a queue to warm my bed.'

He looked at her for a moment, assessing, as if he knew she was desperate to loose her tongue upon him, before taking pity on her and granting the boon of speech. 'You may give me your thoughts, precious,' he said, and his patronising tone said it knew exactly what she was about to lavish upon him.

She did not disappoint. 'I am not one of them,' she spat with such venom it would have made a viper proud. 'I do not want to share your bed. I do not want your horrible hands anywhere near me, and I will always, *always* be looking for a way to kill you. You'll develop a twitch because of me, Martinet.' She returned his grin, in the most unpleasant fashion she could muster.

'A twitch? And why would I be developing one of those, sweet pea? Do tell?' It was obvious he found her antics terribly amusing and it was all he could do not to burst out laughing.

'Because you'll be permanently looking over your shoulder.' Her teeth snapped shut together on the last syllable, indicating she meant business.

He snorted in amusement though, which diffused her tough statement somewhat. 'I'll have you dribbling at my feet in no time, Violetta. I have a one hundred percent success rate with women and I don't expect you will prove the exception to the rule. You may take a while to train, but you'll get there eventually; on your hands and knees of course.'

She hissed at him and her violet eyes loomed larger than life in her head, framed by her beautifully pale, porcelain skin. The urge to do some irreparable damage to any part of his anatomy was upon her, but unfortunately, without the use of her body it left her strangely helpless and she didn't like the feeling one little bit.

'Feeling vulnerable for the first time in a very long time, Violetta?'

He gave her a disparaging glance and turned his back upon her. His shoulders were drawn in a tight line, and if she didn't know better she would say the man was furious. There were a few interminable seconds of silence and trapped inside her body, motionless and once again mute, real fear began to consume her. Oh yes, she held a few priceless drops of holy water in her hands, but the chance that she might ever be able to use them was slim. Questions began to pour through her brain as adrenaline began to overload her system. What did he want with her? Would she be constantly bound? Did he intend to keep her a prisoner? Would he really *use* her in the way he had implied? How did she get herself out of this awful mess with her life intact?

'My brothers and sisters felt fear too, Vi.' She should have been glad that the silence had been broken, but his slow, almost disembodied voice would have made her quiver in horror, had that option been available to her. The loathing and contempt she felt emanating from his back was pure and unadulterated hatred, and it was all for her. 'Not just fear, of course,' he continued, 'there was also terror and shock as you came at them with your many implements and varied methods of death. Some were quick and merciful, but others were dragged out with a good deal more vigour, weren't they Violetta?'

It was a strangely odd thing to be glad that you could not use your voice, but she had to admit that being unable to answer that particular question was a good thing. 'Oh, don't worry your pretty little head about it. I'll never require an answer of you. But I do wonder as to why you dragged some of those deaths out and bloodied your instruments with far more enthusiasm than absolutely necessary. One could almost gather you were beginning to enjoy yourself, meeting out those latter deaths.'

Having someone read your every thought was as disconcerting as it was annoying. How could these vampires cope with this kind of intensely personal interaction, day in, day out? It would drive you crazy.

'Ahh, so now you're beginning to understand my world. Are you looking forward to becoming a part of it?'

She made him wait for her answer. If she was to be marooned inside the shell her body had become, then there was no rush to respond to his taunts. Letting her ears prick up she heard soft strains of Strauss as they seeped in porous lines from the large windows and doors that had been left open wide to cool the occupants within. The night air did little to freshen her body. Martinet had the most peculiar effect upon her. Not liking the direction her train of thought was taking, she decided he had waited long enough. Her answer was short and to the point: *Go to hell.* Although her voice was still trapped deep within her larynx she didn't miss his answering laughter. She was glad she could be such a source of amusement for him.

He released his hold on her abruptly and, having been put hopelessly off balance, she stumbled to the ground. The jarring jolt had twin tears flowing from her eyes. His pain management had ceased, apparently.

'You're going to look so beautiful, splayed out on my bed this evening, chérie. Should I use the soft black rope to tie you up or would you prefer the harsh, metal cuffs?' He appeared to consider the matter. 'Hmm, the cuffs I think, because seeing your wrists adorned with the marks of my possession would be very satisfying. Every time you moved, the gentle pain of their chafing would remind you of me.' He gave her a wolfish grin.

Gritting her teeth Violetta tried to summon up a sneeringly derisive reply, but the pain of her fractured limb was making all normal thought process virtually impossible. If he had not brought her to her knees of his own accord, her shoulder would have taken her legs out from under her regardless. Neurons fired and sizzled within her brain, screaming morphine for the most part, and for once in her life she was rendered speechless. If Martinet knew the level of her current agony he made no show of the fact, for he carried on with his delightful bedtime story, obliviously.

'When I get you back to my humble abode, Vi, should I strip you like a lover, gently removing every single piece of annoying frippery that mars the beauty of that truly amazing body beneath it - or should I be rough? Would you like that? I could rip, tear, rend, pop and sever; buttons and zippers would not stand a chance, lace would melt under my fist and that stunningly gorgeous and ridiculously see-through dress you're wearing would be history. A pity, perhaps, but on the plus side you won't be required to wear clothes under my roof. During your initial training you will remain naked at all times and this will help both of us understand your body and its reactions, in order to maximise and prolong both elements of pleasure and pain. Pleasure will be your reward for good behaviour and pain will be my reward if you decide to flaunt the rules.'

Violetta heard his threats, somewhere in the midst of the agony-filled void her body had entered, and she automatically bared her teeth and growled in response. The reflex was shockingly unladylike, even for her, but it was as instinctive and unstoppable as a force nine gale. 'I will not share your bed,' she managed to grind out, but even as she uttered the words she knew them to be a lie. Escape from this monster would be a miracle and one, for all her many talents, that she might not be capable of.

'Your body has already submitted itself into my care. I suspect your mind will take some convincing, but where the body leads...' The sound of his annoying laughter, ringing out loudly in the night air, got her back to her feet when little else would have managed the task. Glaring at him, with eyes full of fire and hatred, she once again found her voice.

'Do you think that chaining me to your bed will bring them back? Venting your perversions upon me will sully their memories, surely?' Her words were bitter and she almost chewed and swallowed them whole in her resentment of him.

'Oh, if only that were possible, chérie, but my soul is so black that even were you capable of such a deed, my forgiveness would not necessarily follow. I find myself attracted to you in the worst possible way and seeing as how I've witnessed, in my mind's eye, every single death you've meted out to my brethren, helpless to do anything other than watch the contempt and brutality that you have shown our race, I find the prospect of bringing you low a very tantalising one. Training you to become a wanton, shameless servant, who will be desperate for the slightest touch of my hand, is a heartily appealing project. The pièce de résistance, I think, will be making you fall in love with me - for that would be the ultimate revenge. When the fear, hate and loathing have all worn off, and I've made you into a docile, adoring little thing, you'll be forever tied to me, knowing that your feelings will never be returned. Ah, just think, chérie, you'll be trapped in your own personal living hell and it will be utterly inescapable.' He sighed theatrically and said, 'Cue Romeo and Juliette, and the biggest tragedy of all ages. Except that I won't be killing myself anytime soon. You'll have to off yourself and be content with a mini catastrophe.'

Violetta had listened to his ridiculous tirade in disbelief. Who did this vamp think he was? The odds of her falling in love with him were about the same as her suddenly growing wings and sprouting a shiny gold halo: non-existent. She knew what he was and that in itself would be enough to ensure she remained forever distant.

Letting him hear her thoughts, enunciating them carefully in her mind one by one so he could feel their full benefit, she carefully orchestrated a distraction, whilst her good wrist prepared to do its worst. This is what she had been trained for - remaining strong and calm in the face of adversary. She would win this battle, for she could not afford to lose.

In a single fluid move the contents of her vial exploded in a thousand teardrops, like a fractured sheet of glass, almost invisible in the velvet black darkness that enveloped them. Monsieur Martinet had danced his last dance. The holy water had taken flight.

Violetta was smart enough not to have looked in the direction she was aiming. If she had, she knew it would have broadcast her intentions to the beast louder than any stray thought might have done. Now that the deed had been completed she raised her head to admire her handiwork and was amazed to find that nothing and no one was in front of her. She wasn't sure what she had expected - blood curdling screams or puffs of hissing smoke - but utter silence and an all-consuming emptiness did not mark a vampires passing, in her opinion. Her fingers grabbed a handful of the damp, sweet-smelling grass from the earth below her and she roared.

'Get out of my head, Martinet. Release me this instant!' His eerily dark laughter confirmed every one of her suspicions. Brought back out of his vision, she found herself still clutching the tube of purified water, but the stopper was still tightly wedged and her body was once again immoveable.

'What, no fist pumping, cheering or loud rejoicing? You disappoint me, chérie. Too bad you can't swear at me.' He blew her a slow and sultry kiss. 'You are going to prove such a delicious challenge. To have you drowning in the sea of love and hanging off my every word as a human would be quite a task all in itself, but to have all of that adoration after I turn you into a vampire tickles me enough that I might decide to give it a shot...'

His words were thankfully cut off as a couple of revellers spilled out onto the stone balcony of the Castello, clutching tall glasses of champagne and waving them around airily in a flirtatious fashion. A tall brunette, wearing a tight black sheath that could almost be called a dress, was baiting her companion.

'There's no one out here, Frederico. It's just the two of us and a sliver of moonlight, how romantic.' The woman giggled and graced him with an exaggerated pirouette. The twirl appeared to be unnecessary, for Frederico's eyes were already popping out of his head. They were currently focused on the soft swell of the brunette's buttocks, which were just about covered by the plunging lines of her dress, but there was plenty more tanned flesh on display if one were slightly disappointed by the fact. The whole of her back was exposed and sheer panels of fabric revealed most of her waist and midriff. Being blessed with a tall and willowy frame which was currently balanced on spike heels, the woman had a silhouette that any Bond girl would be proud of.

'Do you want to kiss me?' She purred her question seductively, but apparently did not require an answer for she was already bending her neck forward in an inviting manner. Frederico needed no further encouragement, and with eyes drunk with lust he plunged his hands through the brunette's hair and pulled her close for some lipstick stealing action. Judging by the ferocity of his kiss, Violetta suspected that he had been tormented and teased for some time.

'Lovely evening for a stroll, Duchess.' Martinet's voice, sharp and sardonic, broke the lovers' embrace abruptly. There was a shocked gasp, a twist of an elegantly aristocratic head and a glint of light upon a slightly elongated canine.

Violetta wanted to scream. Castello Verde was full of the undead this evening, and here she was, one of the most famed vampire huntresses of all time, having been rendered more helpless than a baby. She could not even utter a sound.

'Damn you, Martinet. You are disturbing my dinner plans, wouldn't you know.' A long pink tongue darted out to caress her fang before she took a deep, calming breath. 'But I see I am disturbing you also. What have you got there, Michel? A tasty young morsel with which to do your worst? Perhaps we should share?' The mischief and malic combined in her voice put the fear of God into Violetta and if they hadn't, the duchess' next words would have.

'I've heard you like to make a mess of them. Blood and gore everywhere, isn't that right, darling?'

Violetta wanted to cover her ears and scream. Was this to be the end of her short-lived career? Ripped apart under the cover of darkness by two mean-minded, bloody-thirsty vamps?

'Sorry, Maggie, but you'll have to search out other avenues of amusement this evening. I have plans for this one. Lots of plans.'

The Duchess' eyes narrowed and her eyes sought out Violetta, pinpointing her with perfect clarity in the almost non-existent light.

'Ahhh, wait a moment. Isn't this the little huntress you've been seeking,

Violetta Cancellaro?'

'Cancellaro.' He smiled and rolled the word about on his tongue as if testing it for authenticity. It suited her. 'Yes, I believe it is,' came the ironic reply. 'As it happens she walked right into my lap, trying to kill me, of course.'

The Duchess' hand shot up to cover her face as she smothered a snort of amusement. When she had managed to get herself back under control she said, 'You know that the odds were two to one as to whether you'd make it through tonight alive?' Her eyes twinkled with mirth.

'I had heard the figure mentioned, oh ye of little faith.' He gave her a faintly mocking look and winked.

'Oh, don't look at me. I told them there wasn't a woman alive who could take you down. They all fall panting at your feet, don't they, Michel? Out of curiosity though, now that you have her, what are you going to do with her? Plate her up and suck her dry?'

Violetta really wished they wouldn't speak about her as if she were already dead. It was slightly demoralising, to say the least. From the expression on the Duchess' face it was clear that she assumed Violetta's days were numbered and of the single digit variety.

'No. I'm going to play with her. We have a little score to settle. If she proves to be entertaining I might even keep her for a pet.'

The Duchess clapped her hands together. 'Divine. You really are the monster they say you are - how wonderfully enchanting. And to think I didn't believe them at first.' She shook her head in awe. 'You do know she's untouched? I can almost smell her virgin blood from here.' She raised an eyebrow and gave Martinet a look of pure devilment.

He gave Violetta a measuring look. 'Surely not,' he mused to himself, taken aback for a moment. Chewing on a finger thoughtfully he turned his attention back to the Duchess and said, 'Don't worry, I've had my fair share of breaking-in virgins; she'll be completely unsafe with me.' Having said his piece he looked down, and then frowned. Frederico had sunk to his knees in front of the Duchess and his tongue was practically hanging out of his mouth. His eyes lolled at awkward angles and his hands flapped around uselessly in his lap. It wasn't a particularly pretty sight.

'Maggie, sort him out, poor boy,' he admonished her.

The Duchess, who had all but forgotten the tasty little after-dinner treat she had brought along for the evening, cast her gaze down upon Frederico and bit her lip. 'Oops,' she said, most unapologetically, followed by, 'damn it, Michel; I find I have almost lost my appetite for the pathetic human in light of all this new excitement. Can I watch you instead? You know how I love to watch them being broken-in, so to speak.' She pouted prettily and raised her beguiling eyes up to his, utilising their full force. She was aware that they would have practically no effect on him, but any small advantage was better than none.

'She's a killer, Maggie. I wouldn't hang around if I were you. If I have a lapse of concentration she'd dice me up in a second.'

Damn right, thought Violetta, who would have loved to do some pretty fast dicing in less than a second, given half a chance.

19

Martinet ignored the snide comment and directed his next sentence towards the Duchess. 'Did you know that Lachlan had more holes in him than a Krispy Kreme donut store after she'd finished with his body? She's callous, brutal, fast and exceptionally cunning. I'd cut your losses, if I were you. Even though I have her utterly shut down and helpless over there, she's still clutching her tube of holy water, just waiting for an opportunity to throw it all over me.'

The Duchess did not seem at all perturbed by his warning and Martinet suspected he had said exactly the wrong thing to her, which was immediately confirmed when she said, 'How perfectly wonderful,' and clapped her hands together in glee. What was it with women?

'Just think of the fun you can have with her,' she gushed. 'You can break the chit down piece by piece and mess around with her.' The Duchess closed her eyes, tipped her face heavenwards towards the abundance of brilliant stars and inhaled a large breath of the fragrant night air. 'I love Venice,' she murmured, as her eyes slanted seductively. 'I love the romance, the history, the sights, the smells - but most of all, I love its utter absurdity. A city built on stilts! It hasn't changed much in six hundred years, but I guess you knew that.' She sucked in another portion of the sweetly scented air. 'I adore gardenias, almost as much as I adored my maker and every sordid little detail of my training he required me to complete. Alas, he's been dead over two hundred years and no matter where I turn, the sex has never been the same.'

'Are you offering, Maggie? I'm sure I have a slot you can have somewhere before Christmas.'

The Duchess gave a little grunt of amusement. 'Very funny,' she giggled. 'You're a man-whore, if such a term can be used for our kind. I wouldn't go near you with somebody else's barge pole, even if it was twenty foot long.'

'You'd love to go near me, Maggie, and we both know it. The power that I might wield over you is what keeps you away.' He raised his eyebrows and stared straight through her.

'Yes, that too, but I need someone to stand faithfully at my side. I always have. You're not tormented by the same troubles, are you, Michel? I, for one, miss the bond of maker and slave, the fundamental power exchange and my complete and utter submission to his every syllable. He was from Venice, of course, back in the days when there was plenty of trade to be had in spices, silk and grain.' The Duchess shook her head as if to free it from the memories of an age long past before directing her lidded gaze towards Frederico. Tapping him on the head gently, she whispered, 'Sleep.' His eyes immediately closed and he slumped to the ground in a stupor, his limbs tangling beneath him. 'Well, that's my problem taken care of,' she said with a cheeky smile. 'Now let's see how you deal with yours.' She looked at him expectantly and batted her eyelids.

Martinet gave her an exasperated look and waved his hands about with an air of annoyance. 'Isn't there something else you'd rather be...?' he was cut-off mid-sentence.

'No, absolutely nothing,' said the Duchess, almost dribbling with the prospect of some good old-fashioned entertainment. 'Please let me watch,' she begged. 'I haven't had this much fun in centuries.'

'You need to get out more,' said Martinet, rolling his eyes, already knowing there was little chance that he would get rid of her. 'Fine, if you can stand the threat of death by sainted water, you may watch. To be honest, I'm intrigued about your virgin theory. What say we give her an orgasm and test the waters?'

The Duchess giggled delightedly in response. 'Oh goodness, you're just as evil as they say you are. How perfectly wonderful.' She was already shuffling backwards, away from the soft spill of light from the Castello's heavy wooden doors and into the darkness beyond. 'Please don't let me distract you. I'll stand in the shadows over here, while you go do your thing.' Making a show of smoothing the skirt of her expertly tailored dress, the Duchess backed away towards the dull grey stones of the walled garden, so she would remain hidden away from view.

Martinet rolled his eyes and muttered softly under his breath, 'Women.' They were the bane of his several lifetimes.

'I heard that, Michel.'

'You were meant to,' he replied with an overly sweet, dulcet tone. 'I know how sensitive those ears are, Maggie. And whilst on the subject, can you make sure we have no more unannounced visitors? I want no annoying humans deciding to take a midnight stroll right now. I need my wits about me.'

'Already got the problem in hand, darling,' she replied, waving a beautifully long black velvet opera glove in his direction. Sinking back into the dark gloom, the Duchess then disappeared from view entirely.

Having been given centre stage with an attentive audience, Martinet found himself somewhat reluctant to humiliate the girl. That in itself was crazy, as he intended to do far worse to her in the next few weeks, and it would make a mostly fully-clothed, public orgasm seem like child's play in comparison. He was going to strip her of all she knew, manipulate her actions, hormones and thoughts until she didn't even know herself any more. She would become his slave in every sense of the word, and not only that, she would come to adore him. She would be what was termed as 'one of Martinet's women'. She would vie for his attention, be trained to please him and only him, and respond to his every command. He wanted her utterly helpless under his hand - as his coven had been under hers. Would he kill her? Perhaps. There was always the slim chance that she might kill him first, but that simply added fuel to a fire already blazing wildly out of control. It was a challenge he could not resist. If she proved to be tempting enough and passed the relevant tests, he would change her. He cared not for her thoughts or feelings on the matter. He would rule her body with an iron fist that showed no mercy and he would rule her mind as a dictator. She would have no choice but to obey. He couldn't wait to see the initial fear, loathing and hatred that would be reflected in her eyes, knowing that before long he would change it to drugged desire, adulation and simpering obedience. She would be his little pet. One who would pant for him while he was near, and pine for him when he was not. His revenge would be all the sweeter as she knew exactly what he intended and would be fighting him every step of the way. He wished her luck. Now it was time to show her who was boss and hopefully reveal one or two secrets in the process...

He had to admit that curiosity had got the better of him. A twenty-four year old virgin? It was surely an impossibility in this day and age, but the Duchess was rarely wrong in these matters. If she was, he mused, it would put a decidedly wonderful slant on things. Deflowering virgins was one of the most delectable pastimes known to his kind. If she had absolutely no knowledge of sex, he could mould her exactly as he wished because she would have no preconceived ideas on the subject. If the huntress could be tamed, and that was by no means a likely outcome, if she was virginal, his job would be made considerably easier by the fact. The time had come to test the waters.

'Bend over, Violetta.'

Orgasmic

As he issued the command, Martinet gave her back her voice and allowed her to form facial expressions once more. This was for his benefit, rather than hers. He wanted to watch her reactions and study every nuance of each emotion that might choose to cross her face. He wanted to know everything about her. This was not due to undying curiosity on his part, but a need to store every single detail about her that he could later use against her. It would all be filed neatly in his own personal arsenal of data and his photographic memory would have no problem recalling the information as and when it was needed. To what ends he hoped to achieve by this remained to be seen - perhaps it would come in useful in order to persuade her to do something, or maybe as a bargaining chip for her cooperation at some point. He didn't have a problem with blackmail, either, if the purpose suited him. He was nothing if not ruthless in his dealings with humans.

Movement caught the corner of his eye and he turned to watch her body bend over smoothly from the waist. She did not stop moving until she rested at a near perfect ninety degree angle. It was a good spanking angle. He knew, because he'd tested the theory on many occasions. The expression that now featured on her face, due mostly to her automatic obedience to his command, was priceless. It was a cross between murderous rage and hideous embarrassment. He noted how her cheeks had flooded with colour at being so easily manipulated and it gave him cause to wonder. The next command he issued should take the guesswork out of the equation.

'Lift your skirt up, chérie, and display that beautiful backside of yours.'

She summarily exploded, like a can of coke that had taken a vigorous ride on a pogo stick. Score one for the Duchess, he thought.

'How dare you!' Violetta's violet eyes went a dangerous shade of purple and she shrieked her displeasure at him. 'Is this how you get your kicks? Issuing stupid commands and ogling bottoms? You are insane!'

Martinet had to bite his bottom lip quite hard to keep from smiling at her fraught response. Of course, she had no option but to pick up the hem of her floor length lilac frock and pull the entire length of it up, over her back. Her rump was now blatantly on display for his perusal and it was even more beautiful than he had imagined. The cherry on top was that her face had darkened to a beautifully deep scarlet. There was little doubt about the matter now and the Duchess had been right on the money.

'Very nice,' he commented appreciatively, knowing it would rile her. He wasn't lying though. The view was magnificent. Although the human eye would have been able to see very little about five metres away from the Castello's grand oak doors, his were able to spot the tiniest of details, even from the respectable distance he held himself at.

For instance, he could tell from the washing tag that her gown needed to be laundered by specialist dry-cleaners. She'd left the thing hanging out of the back of her dress and would probably be mortified if she found out. The tag also told him that it could not be ironed. It was all thoroughly exciting stuff. He also knew that pale, white, Egyptian cotton had been used to trim her dress and that the method used to complete the task was a blind hem stitch. He would put money on the fact that her satin bikini panties had been designed by Calvin Klein even though the waistband had been twisted and the only lettering visible was a 'C'. It helped that he'd studied ladies underwear in great detail over the years. From La Perla to Victoria's Secret, he'd seen it and stripped it, from more than his fair share of willing participants, too.

'Slide your panties down your ankles.' The command was issued in a silky voice. He was well aware that that particular order would have her frothing at the mouth and he was not to be disappointed. The look she gave him could have killed a mortal.

'Why are you doing this?' There was a hiccup and a soft sob. The distress in her voice was most pleasing.

'Because I can,' he replied, and watched with avid enjoyment while she peeled her delicate underwear slowly down her smooth, long legs. It took a little longer than it would have normally, due to her broken arm, which he allowed to hang limply by her side for the time being. From early on in their relationship he intended to define, quite clearly, that good behaviour meant pleasure and that bad behaviour had such dire consequences that it wasn't worth thinking about.

He would fix her arm later, if she pleased him. It would take him a few minutes, but after he'd finished it would be impossible to tell she'd ever broken it. Knitting bones together and threading nerves, sinew and fibres back into the right slots was not difficult for him. Earning the reward of that boon, however, would be horribly difficult for her. Violetta was going to quickly learn that exemplary conduct would earn her rewards, but naughty behaviour would ensure that humiliations and punishments would be heaped upon her. It mattered not to him which path she chose, he would probably have equal fun with either. He frowned. Scrap that thought. He'd have far more fun if she disobeyed his every word and fought like a hell cat. He was counting on it.

When the panties began to slide down towards her ankles he took a moment to savour the anger and fury she directed at him. He knew her mind was rebelling against his absolute control, but she had yet to find an override switch for his commands - nor would she. Once he was inside a mind there was no way, to his knowledge, that he could be removed. As soon as he had a little of her blood inside him the bond would become even more pronounced and it would grow stronger with each subsequent feeding. The sooner he drank from her the better, because then there would be no going back. They would be intrinsically bound and then, there was only death or rebirth to consider.

He smiled as he felt her mind give a little push towards his. She was already raging mad and struggling for all she was worth to try and stop the inevitable progress of her flimsy undergarments, but she would soon learn that resistance against him was hopelessly futile. When her panties finally piled in a pretty little puddle at her feet she was beside herself with mortification. Her modesty was wonderfully enchanting. He watched her squirm. He was beginning to wonder why he hadn't tried this revenge game earlier. If he'd known how much fun it would be he could have been at it for centuries...

'Each time you try to fight me, chérie, I shall make things a little more difficult for you. That way you'll soon come to realise that obedience is the only option worth considering.' His tongue licked his lips thoughtfully. 'Let's see. Hmm, I suppose I had better check whether you're aroused before I get carried away.'

He approached her slowly, his soft leather brogues making no noise on the verdant carpet of short grass beneath him. He purposefully took his time. He wanted her to feel each one of his silent steps, knowing that she would just about be able to watch him from the corner of her eye. He knew her heartrate was at its maximum setting and that her mouth had run so dry she was unable to swallow. He also knew heat had begun to pool between her legs, fiery liquid heat that had nothing to do with his exceptionally clever talents - and yet everything to do with him. Either she found him charmingly attractive or she was turned on by his dominant behaviour. It was probably a combination of the two, but there was no denying her body's response. Good. If she found him attractive, it would make things easier for him and much more humiliating for her.

'Are you wet for me, Princess?' With his final step he reached the beautiful, twin peaks of her buttocks and drew his hand leisurely across them, with the lightest of touches. He noted that they were firm, taut specimens and that they wobbled in all the right places. After a few moments he pursed his lips and decided she was not going to answer his question. How terribly rude! Squeezing one of her delectable ass cheeks sharply he was rewarded with a gasp. It appeared she hadn't lost her tongue, after all.

'Answer the question.' His tone was abrupt.

'Fuck you,' she whispered in a panicked, thready voice.

So, the huntress was losing her edge. What a pity. He knew that if he let his control of her slip her legs would buckle out from under her. The girl was scared.

'Oh, you will be precious, if we can tame the huntress out of you. Now answer the question or I'll make you answer it, and believe me when I say you won't like my tactics.' His voice was a seductive murmur and he let it penetrate her entire body. By the way her teeth clenched tightly together, he guessed she didn't much like the effect he had on her. Too bad.

He decided to go easy, just this once, and give her an opportunity to speak. He waited. A long, pregnant pause lit up the night sky and the tension around them had a torque a Mercedes would have been proud of. She was in a spin and there was no right way to turn. As he suspected, no answer was forthcoming. Her lips remained held in a tight line and she would not look at him. He had never considered, even for a moment, that there would be, which was why she had been positioned exactly like this, her buttocks thrust up in the air and bared for his hands. Licking his lips, he felt a glimmer of excitement begin to stir within him. He had not felt such a powerful sentiment since the death of Jacques de Molay, the Grand Master of the Templar Knights, who had been burned at the stake in 1314. Also a vampire, Molay had been a close friend and confederate during some of Martinet's more 'unstable' years. His ugly death had nearly been the end of him, but that was another story. Thankfully, the subject matter today was a far more palatable emotion.

'Oh, Violetta,' he sighed delightedly. 'You and I are going to get along splendidly.' With no further ado he began unfastening the thick leather belt from around his waist. He didn't hurry. He took his own sweet time as he wanted her to hear what he was doing. The chink of metal as the clasp became free, the swish of movement as it slithered through the loopholes of his trousers and a final, slow drag as he unthreaded the tongue. She was a smart lady. He knew she'd quickly put two and two together and would realise exactly what he had planned for her. He casually glanced her way, and although he was eagerly awaiting her reaction, not a whit of it was reflected upon her face. He looked at her with a lazy, bored expression and voiced his next question.

'Do you want to run, Violetta?' His voice was a dangerously low drawl. He gave her mind an extra hard push to make sure she answered him this time. He knew she felt it, because her head snapped back in shock. Yeah, and that's only the half of it, sweet pea, he thought.

'Yes,' she whispered, and there was a hint of vulnerability in her voice. She wasn't lying, not that she would have been able to. He could feel her body trying to prime itself for flight, but that avenue was not open to her. To be fair, just about all avenues were locked down and closed, but it would take her some time to realise that and get used to his omnipotent presence. He would look forward to the day she gave up fighting him, but suspected that once it happened her appeal would dwindle significantly. He wasn't going to let the thought concern him; there was always death for her to look forward to.

'So, are you going to answer my earlier enquiry? Are you wet for me, precious?' He began to double the belt over in his fist, forming a slanted 'O' shape and tapped it against his palm a few times for good measure. Meanwhile he watched her lips intently and waited for them to move.

'Oh, I believe I already did,' she murmured, and smiled sweetly at him. The shock of her cheeky riposte nearly, oh so nearly, made his breath catch. So she had been playing with him? Unheard of. The fighting hellcat was back. How exquisite.

'I can make you answer me in a polite fashion the easy way or the hard way,' he said, before unleashing his killer smile.

'You'd better get used to the hard way, then,' she said, letting her violet eyes bore into his.

Martinet bent his neck to the left until he heard it crack. This one had plenty of cheek, and in more than one area. Clearing his throat noisily he said, 'Good. I much prefer the hard way. But you do realise this might hurt, chérie? What with that poor arm of yours, I'd have thought you might want to play it safe.' The mocking words dripped from a honeyed tongue.

'I'm a huntress,' came the sharp retort. 'We're taught to handle pain. She glared at him with wonderfully narrowed eyes and her pupils were so large they nearly obscured her pretty, violet irises. 'I've had vampire talons sink their wrath into my back, arms, legs and breasts. Fangs have tried repeatedly to sever prominent arteries in my neck and thighs. Fists have broken my nose and bruised my ribs.

Nothing you can do with your belt will compel me to answer the question. I can withstand a great deal of torture.'

Martinet merely smiled. It had been a magnificent speech, but it had little merit upon the methods he was likely to use. He decided to re-educate her on the matter. 'Ah, but this isn't going to be the same kind of torture you're used to, chérie. This will be a mix of pleasure and pain, and when we combine the two I think that pretty pink tongue of yours will start telling me all sorts of secrets, without my having to search for them.'

She didn't deign to respond to him, but her eyes, those gloriously vivid eyes, told him all he needed to know. This was a battle she expected to win. Little did she know, but there wasn't a female in the land who'd managed to best him at this game and she wasn't going to be the first.

A faint buzzing noise entered his sphere of hearing and distracted him for a moment. He couldn't help but watch the slow, meandering path of a lone mosquito with his eagle-eyed vision. The insect had obviously spotted some fresh, juicy flesh that would almost certainly bear a tasty reward and was homing in for the kill. Entertainingly enough, with regards to mosquitoes, it was the female of the species who did the damage and readily sought out the blood of humans. She needed it in order to lay her eggs. Unfortunately for Violetta, in the land of the undead it was the male bloodsuckers who wreaked the most havoc. The hungry beastie landed with skilled precision on her right buttock and prepared to take a long, soothing drink of the red stuff. Reaching forward with his index finger and thumb, his lightning-fast reflexes squashed the unfortunate soul between his fingers. No one was going to have the honour of dining from her before he had taken his fill. Whilst the chit aroused him sexually, it was the thought of taking her blood which really excited him, not least because he knew that his taking of her blood would destroy her - if not physically, certainly emotionally. As soon as he had ingested some of her precious nectar she would be a huntress no more, for his venom would forever live inside her. Her downfall was all he lived for these days and the irony did not escape him. Revenge kept him motivated in a way nothing else could.

Turning his attention back to the belt in his hands, he caressed the supple leather and inhaled the faint scent of tobacco it had managed to acquire over the years. It was his favourite, and he suspected that after today's events it might rise even further in his estimation. Hell, he might have to frame the thing. With that thought uppermost in his mind he tightened his grip and set his sights on his mark; the sumptuous curve of her ass.

Giving her no warning whatsoever he brought the strap down. A loud crack resonated through the night air, followed by a shocked gasp. Giving her a minute to process the stinging slap, he ran a single finger down the line he had made. His huntress tried to remain stoic and bit down on her lip, not wanting to give him the pleasure of hearing her moan. Little did she know, but he wasn't going to stop until he heard her scream in pleasure, so he wasn't in the least bit worried about her holding back a few petulant whimpers.

Bringing the belt back up, he let his hand feel the long length of worn leather in an almost reverent fashion. He knew she had bitten her lip in order not to cry out, but it was early days yet.

He counted to three and let the belt fly once again. It was another sharp slap and this time he was rewarded with a hiss. He pressed his fingertips down into the fresh pink stripe to see if he'd done the job properly. She gave him a strangled moan, which she cut off almost as soon as she had uttered it, but it was enough. Giving her no time to recover her wits, he let the belt loose one more time.

When the belt sank its teeth into her ass for the third time he managed to get a curse out of her. It was a pretty innocuous one, but he suspected she'd get more inventive the longer he continued. For now he allowed her a small break to compose herself, while he feasted his eyes upon her striped rear. Three blazing lines were beginning to surface, and knowing he was the one who had put them there was very satisfying indeed.

'Did they sting, precious?' He didn't receive an answer to his query, but it hardly mattered as he already knew the answer. Just to make sure, he ran a hand over one of the blossoming streaks of pale pink flesh. Hearing the strangled invective she tried so hard to hide was music to his ears.

'Now I shall find out if that nubile body of yours is hot for mine. You just stand there, while I go check, chérie. At her infuriated roar he chuckled and to fuel the flames of her ire, he placed both of his very talented hands down upon her; hands that knew how to play a woman. They could perform a slow, sensuous rhumba or a fast and intense salsa, for that matter they could execute the whole of Rachmaninov's third piano concerto, if he were so inclined, but for tonight it would have to be short and sweet. They had an agenda to complete and he wanted her to be firmly secreted away in his mountain mansion before the sun released its potent morning rays upon them.

Letting his fingers walk up the insides of her splayed legs, he bent over slowly and pressed his soft lips into one of the rosy stripes. The mewl she emitted was choked and confused. She knew it should have hurt, but was surprised when the sensation was actually quite pleasant. Violetta had a lot to learn about her body and he would be more than happy to teach her. He was going to have a double dose of fun with this one. He would train her to slather at his feet first as a human, before rebirthing her in his own image as a vampire, that which she despised and hated. Then he could have the ultimate revenge - for the huntress would become the hunted. Maybe he could even give those friends of hers a call to finish her off. It would be a fitting demise for his most hated enemy, killed by those she once loved.

Letting his teeth scrape along the raised line of the belt mark, he began to slide his hands further up her legs. His hands moved with teasing leisureliness, his fingers rubbing little swirls into the wonderfully yielding flesh of her supple, inner thighs. He smiled as he felt her jaws clamp down upon a soft little moan of pleasure. He had a feeling she wouldn't manage to keep those delightful little sounds hidden for much longer. Working gradually towards his goal, his fingers luxuriated in the soft mass of red curls he found at the apex of her sex. It had been a barely there kiss of his fingertips but he knew she felt it as he'd let himself seep into her mind. He also knew she would have given anything to escape his wandering fingers, and that, in his eyes, made the torment far more gratifying.

Cupping her sex and cradling the heat he found there was an almost divine experience. There was another hiss and she gave him a baleful glare, but he wasn't the least bit interested in her face. Two of his fingers formed a two-pronged fork and were aiming for her labia, doling out tiny little flutters of movement. They then progressed to a firmer intensity before he began caressing the lips intently, feeling them swell underneath his fingertips.

Interestingly enough, when he was anchored in the minds of most humans he found a need to distance himself from the constant babble of chatter they felt necessary to process on an almost endless basis. Inane, useless chatter for the most part, which could drive a lesser man insane. With Violetta, however, he found himself wanting to know what she was thinking, what she felt at each touch he might choose to bestow upon her, and he wanted to be there, inside her, when she reached that magical pinnacle that would force her to lose some of that rigid control that she tried so hard to maintain.

His forked fingers dipped into the valley that surrounded her clitoris and performed and intimate dance that would do little but frustrate her. He slid forward and back, again and again, until he detected in her an urge to buck her hips in time with his delicate ministrations. Allowing her the privilege of that one small movement, knowing that the action would madden, humiliate and tease her senseless, he continued on the warpath he had forged. Employing soft, sinuous caresses to some of the more intimate parts of her body, he knew it wouldn't take long before her voice would resurface. Whether she would plead for relief or beg for him to stop remained to be seen, but it would be interesting to find out. In any case, it was time to up the ante. Applying the most delicate touch to the tiny little nub between the apex of her thighs, he waited to see what would happen.

In the end the result was almost comical. Her eyes bulged, her breath caught and she made a gurgling sound in the back of her throat. He could almost feel the pressure behind her eyelids as they burst open in shock. Hearing the enraged expletive that rattled inside her head, unable to find its way out, was most pleasing; but her next words, when she finally managed to get them past the confines of her lips were even better.

'Please stop.' They were a mere whisper of sound, pained and desperate, and truly a delight to behold.

'You mean to tell me that you don't like this?' His voice held a mocking, incredulous tone. Pressing harder with his fingers and working her clit a little faster, he made it clear that he wanted a reply but added a little push for good measure.

'I... I...'

Violetta's head was a jumble of turbulent emotions that were being tossed around in a spin cycle filled with the drug desire. She didn't know which way was up, had no idea what her body was doing or what it might be capable of. Drowning in a sea of tantalising fingers which worshipped her flesh by sliding and slipping everywhere they could, she had no way of fighting him. She was lost.

So, the signs were encouraging, Martinet thought. She had all the markings of an untried, and taking her virginity from her would be the icing on top of an already very chocolaty cake. He was almost bursting with exhilaration at the prospect of her downfall. He wanted to rub his hands in glee. Good grief, it had been years since he'd performed a 'Virgin Conversion', so to speak, and this time he could have some real fun.

'Would you like me to introduce you to the little death, chérie? Watching you dance upon my fingers would be a wonderful sight to behold, would it not?'

'Get. Off. Me.' His lioness roared her malcontent at his treatment of her and he had to bite his lip in order not to laugh out loud and spoil the moment. Keeping his mirth in check was difficult though. Her hips wanted to waggle enticingly, beckoning to be used, her buttocks itched to sway and the ends of her ball-gown looked particularly endearing, wrapped around her ears.

Thrusting a single finger inside her he delighted in the fact that it was immediately coated in a sweet, hot, liquid musk. Whilst her level of arousal was hardly breaking news to him, the thin layer of her hymen, which prevented him from extending his long middle finger to its greatest potential, was. How incredible. He could barely believe his luck. Here was a complete novice, absolutely clueless in the ways and workings of love, and he could train her untutored body to please him in any way he chose. A wicked smile lit up his face. The big bad wolf had ensnared Miss Hood, and hell if he wasn't going to eat her, from the inside out. Patience might need to be employed at first, alas, but good things came to those who waited, and he had waited longer than most.

While his finger gently pumped inside her delightfully tiny channel he let his thumb tickle her clit. A few pleasant pulsations to start and then he would begin the fight to the 'little death', for he knew without doubt that she would fight him with everything she had. No matter that she found him extremely attractive or that her body responded in a primal, elemental way to his - she would know exactly what submitting to him would mean: the loss of her family and, most probably, the loss of her life. It would simply make his victory all the sweeter, for she was fighting the inevitable.

Choosing that moment to release his control over her body, he observed that she barely noticed she was once again her own woman. She would figure it out in a few minutes. He wasn't worried. She was too far gone to run, and at this moment in time her body was an instrument of pleasure that only he could play. Letting his thumb state its intentions he moved it faster and harder. Watching her legs, it didn't take long before both her thighs had developed a subtle but noticeable quiver. After another thirty seconds of his 'heaven and back' thumb action it would progress to an earthquake size tremor. The girl was panting, her fists were furled into tight knots and he was surprised she hadn't managed to drop her precious little tube. He knew she still harboured a strong wish to throw it at him, but his fingers could prove very distracting when employed with the right precision.

'Have you ever had an orgasm before, Vi?' This time he didn't voice the question out loud but merely let it echo around a few corners inside her head. It would annoy her more.

'That's none of your goddamn business.' She replied in the same telepathic manner, but with a good deal more volume. Cute. It appeared she was a fast learner. He could only hope her talents would be equally skilful in other areas.

'I don't think you have, Vi, and isn't that the shocker? You have no idea what you've been missing, but the good news is you're about to find out.' His free hand snaked across her chest and reached under the almost transparent lilac organza of her dress. He inveigled his way under the satiny camisole beneath and found a succulent breast hiding between its many folds. His efforts were rewarded as his fingers brushed against a nipple that had already burst free from its protective shell. Closing his fingers around the pointed peak he pulled gently. His body rocked with hers as he felt a heady zing of pleasure shoot straight down to her core. She was close now. It wouldn't take much to send her flying through the gates of delirium. Feeling her struggles beneath him confirmed his suspicions. Legs kicked out, arms flailed and shoulders tried to wrench themselves free of his tight hold - to no avail. He had a vicelike grip upon her and intended to see his little experiment all the way through to the end.

Removing his hand from its very snug resting place, he reached for the belt again. She needed a distraction and this would help. Keeping one hand busy between her legs, he used the belt to rain down soft slaps across her buttocks and thighs. It was an awkward position, but that was the upside of being a vampire. He could hold any position for hours and not feel the slightest bit of discomfort. Well, anywhere except inside his pants, perhaps. There was plenty of discomfort there, and would be for a few days yet, he suspected. He'd have the problem taken care of one way or another.

As her backside came into flower, sporting a beautiful shade of peony pink, he watched her squirm madly to avoid the gentle slaps. They were nothing more than annoyances and there was no real bite to them, but she wouldn't be able to concentrate very carefully while he continued to heap them down upon her. They would help spread a slow burn throughout her body. Keeping up a measured pace and watching as her hips surged forward in pleasure, he monitored her carefully. He attuned himself to her pulse, her blood pressure and her rapidly increasing breathing rate. For a virgin, she was incredibly wet. Trying his hardest to squeeze three of his fingers inside her, he found himself grateful for her copious lubrication. The job wouldn't be nearly as hard as it could have been. Stretching her wide open, with slow little thrusts, he knew there would be a little work involved to get her ready for his cock. When he got her back to his cliff-side palace, or prison, as it would forever remain to her, they'd play about with a few of his toys. Start small and work your way upwards, that was his motto, and his humble home, Oscura Dimora, had quite the collection of toys, and everything else they would need for her training. Or should that be taming?

Her head was a jumble of thoughts. Nothing was particularly coherent. He heard various things of course: her need to avoid the stinging slap of his belt, her wonder at the intense sensations spiralling rapidly out of control inside her, and the powerful hatred she harboured for him and his kind. That last thought he intended to nurture. She'd think he was the anti-Christ by the time he'd finished with her.

His fingers finally sank as far as they could go without taking her precious virginity. They'd save that for later. When Martinet heard her cry out in a keening wave of pleasure as his thumb raced around her clit, he knew it was time. He let the belt fall from his hands and it nestled in the dark grass with barely a sound. Taking from his trouser pocket the small silver dagger he'd misappropriated from her earlier attempt to kill him, he slowly ran the cold length of metal down her arm, gently scoring her flesh, wondering what she would do. If he'd timed the moment accurately enough, and with his fingers doing their worst, she would barely feel it. If he hadn't, she might well snatch the instrument out of his hand and prepare to dance with him. The blade reached her wrist and he pressed the point into her radial artery. Her eyelids fluttered close, but not due to the blade. She hadn't even noticed it. Her whole being was concentrated on one teeny, tiny sexual organ. That suited his purposes perfectly. Running the knife slowly back up the naked flesh of her arm, past her elbow joint, before letting the blade slide over her shoulder blade, he manoeuvred the sharpened point to the carotid artery in her neck. She didn't have a clue what he was doing. The blade did not register at all in her brain and as he neared one of the most important arteries in her body, that which fed the brain with succulently laden, oxygen-rich blood, he could have put an end to her life with one simple slice. It wouldn't be particularly quick or painless, and it would be very messy, but it demonstrated just how breakable humans were and why they shouldn't be messing around with the likes of his kind. He drew the blade back just seconds, a few scant seconds before his huntress would climax, and the urge to kill her was strong. All those deaths she had caused. All those friends she had murdered. His eyes saw a thick curtain of red wash down upon them and he felt himself filled with rage. What a fitting end to her career this would be! A death similar to those she herself had doled out with frightening regularity, and which gave her little cause for remorse. The girl had no conscience apparently, but that was fine because neither did he. He stabbed his blade forward as she began writhing and convulsing underneath his talented fingers. The 'little death' was a fitting term indeed.

Blood

The smell of blood was one of the few things that could make his concentration waver. All vampires could be driven insane with the scent if they were hungry, and he had not fed in over a week. This was not particularly dangerous for one as old as himself, but the urge to tear into Violetta's neck and sink his fangs into the veins beneath was strong. He held himself in check. He had already reigned in the urge to kill the girl, merely stabbing a tiny nick on the top of her shoulder blade, and he was now waiting for the blood to run so he could coat her shiny blade with it. Then she could send her friends home happy in the knowledge that an old coot such as himself had been exterminated from the face of the earth. There would be much rejoicing in the land, although Violetta wouldn't be doing a happy dance any time soon. For one thing her arm was in tatters, and for another, she'd be tied up in his bedroom - awaiting the whims of her captor. Him.

For some reason the area around the shoulder bled particularly well. Perhaps it was due to its proximity to either the brain or the prominent artery in the neck, but in any case, it did not take long before a small river of blood was flowing down her back, and whilst it smelled rather delicious, he really couldn't have that at this moment in time. Using the flat of her blade he liberally coated it in the oozing scarlet ribbons, before dropping it to the ground. The sticky blood wasn't going anywhere, but if he didn't staunch the flow her dress would be ruined, and when she re-entered the ballroom the hunters would know something was amiss. Applying fierce pressure to the entry point of the wound, he cursed when he realised he had stabbed her with a little more force than had been absolutely necessary. He had managed to get carried away in the heat of the moment. He couldn't remember the last time that had happened, but he needed to be careful not to let it happen again or his plans would be for nothing. Feeling his fangs begin to fill his mouth with the intoxicating, metallic tang of blood scenting the air, it wouldn't be long before he could heal her wound. He just needed a couple of seconds. His hunger was so acute that his venom would be released shortly, and he was not to be disappointed. Feeling the first droplet drip down onto his tongue, he scooped his right index finger inside his mouth to collect it. Applying the tiny drop quickly to her puncture wound the blood flow stopped almost instantly. She still had no idea what had happened, but as she turned her newly-awakened, lust-filled eyes around to meet his, he saw her fury there and realised he hadn't managed to achieve his initial objective. In her hand she still had a fierce grip on that bottle of holy water and she was currently preparing to throw it at him. Again. Maybe he wasn't quite as good as he thought he was.

'Stubborn little thing, aren't you?' As her hand raised in the air and her lips began opening in order to vent something loud and unpleasant upon him, his fingers dived back inside her. They'd just have to go for the multiple. She wouldn't be much good for anything after two in a row, but just to make sure he'd lavish her with the full routine this time. Everything he had, he'd throw it at her. This time she wouldn't merely be a puddle on the ground, he'd make sure she was nothing but pulp from head to toe.

Of course, now she'd come down from her post-climactic high, and her faculties were once again firing on all cylinders, she would have realised he'd cut her. It was probably going to have ticked her off a little. When a closed fist full of holy water came flying at him he caught it in mid-strike and felt her arm shake with rage. She'd seen the knife below her, she'd be able to feel the puncture wound on her back, and she wasn't stupid.

It was time to neutralise the situation. Putting her into a relatively simple trance he decided the first place to start was with some hormones, so he liberally sprinkled a bit of testosterone and oestrogen around in her bloodstream. Then he raised her core temperature just a touch and made sure her heartrate didn't slow down. He wanted to keep her in that freshly revved up and gagging-for-sex state. He returned one hand to her nipple and began to tug gently at the teat, while his fingers liberally coated themselves in her ejaculate, of which there was an abundance. Whilst she might not think much of him, her body had decided that he was God. It had responded to his touch and fingers almost instantly and, if anything, her need of him had surprised them both. As he worked her over with gentle strokes in the real world, inside her mind he was about to play dirty. Horribly dirty, he hoped.

Rifling about inside her head, he searched for something he could use. He wanted her secrets, her innermost desires, those naughty little interludes in her mind that she hadn't shared with another living soul. He wanted to find out what made her tick and then send her second hand spinning. It wasn't long before he found something he could use. If he hadn't already discovered that she was a virgin he would have realised it from her complete lack of sexual knowledge. Even her fantasies were relatively tame by anyone's standards, but they could work on that. Give them an inch and they soon wanted a mile. He bent his neck to the left, back to the right and then donned his bow-tie. Plunging into the deepest depths of her head, he was about to act out a scenario that would have her diving headfirst into the big 'O' in spectacular style. The bottle didn't stand a chance.

The Stranger

The hotel lobby was a whirl of electric ceiling fans. The heat was oppressive and there was no relief from the sultry shroud that had fallen down around the milling occupants. Beneath his feet the floor was smooth, glossy and made of teak, whilst the walls were composed of engraved woodwork, comprised of painstakingly chiselled patterns of pretty scrolls and latticework that would have taken several carpenters years to complete. A few stray palm trees dotted the open floor, elegantly swathed in tiny white lights, and a marble fountain took centre stage, spurting out gentle arcs of water and creating a pleasing 'burbling' effect. Large, circular leather sofas in shades of brown and cream were positioned near the bar area, with a few matching ottomans for good measure. A couple of rosewood cabinets, adorned with books, knickknacks and large vases filled to the brim with an eclectic mix of tropical flowers completed the effect. They were many miles from home.

There were no windows to be found in the lobby, but they were hardly needed. Inclement weather was not a common occurrence in the tropics. The lack of them afforded the most magnificent view of the ocean, which currently held itself perfectly still and flat, as if it were lethargic and thoroughly enervated after the intense temperatures of the day.

Martinet lounged indolently against the bar counter. He was dressed for comfort, in lightweight beige slacks, and a white linen shirt which hung open at the neck. As he was going to be undressing himself in short order he didn't want to make things hard on himself. In his hand he cradled a freshly shaken Pina Colada, which was foaming and bubbling over with its enthusiasm to be devoured. Watching the condensation begin to fog the glass, it wasn't long before his fingers were soaked with tiny beads of water. They'd be wet with something else entirely before long, and speaking of 'somethings', here came his delightful étranger, sailing through the wooden double doors and searching for a soft place to land. He immediately turned his back on her and struck up a bland but friendly conversation with the barman. If there was one thing all women hated, it was being studiously ignored.

His disinterest was instantly noted and her eyes had flown over in his direction, slightly taken aback and confused. Violetta was a woman who attracted attention wherever she went, so being swiftly dismissed was not something she was used to. She had a tall, almost regal body, finely honed limbs, a beautiful English rose complexion and hair that could set the world on fire with its red, seething flames. Discretely admiring her from the mirror's reflection that ran all the way along the back of the bar, Martinet had the sudden urge to bury his hands in the auburn inferno and twist ropes of her silky hair around his fingers, inhaling her scent and flooding his senses with her unique perfume. It annoyed him. He wished he did not find her quite so attractive. Hopefully he would become inured to her charms in short order, or his libido was going to have a marvellously entertaining time as he completed his numerous games of revenge.

In the far corners of his acute peripheral vision, he devoured her. When he'd initially turned his back on her she'd almost stopped in her tracks, slightly shocked at his abrupt behaviour, but she quickly managed to regain her composure. She shouldn't feel too bad. She had the complete and adoring attention of the barman, who was now only half-listening to the conversation he was carrying on, judging by his monosyllabic answers, and he couldn't say he blamed him. Violetta was dressed to kill. He should know. This might have been her fantasy initially, but he had most certainly embellished parts of it - to his complete and eminent satisfaction.

She was garbed in a laid-back, dark-brown silk number that flaunted a little bit of lace and a few tiers of ruffles in all the right places. It gave her a carefree vibe, but it certainly didn't have the same effect on him. The ruffles stopped upon her upper thighs, the cut-out lace panels gave tempting glimpses of flesh just above her full breasts, and the strappy crystal sandals she wore shot her body up to heights unknown. He wanted his hands up her skirt, his mouth suckling just below those lacy wisps of fabric and her feet bare - along with the rest of her. Next time he played out these kinds of fantasies he'd make sure she was naked from the word go. It would save time and angst. Namely his angst, but he was the important party here in any case.

Watching her check out his backside as she sauntered towards him, he observed that she wasn't displeased with his physique. His rejection of her initial advance hadn't dampened her spirits in any way, shape or form. Carrying her little clutch bag carefully under one arm, her stance stiffened and her eyes hardened. She was preparing for battle. The violet eyes roamed over him carefully, and unless he was mistaken, she liked what she saw.

He'd discovered over the years that women had certain qualities they wanted from prospective partners, and up there in the top five was the need for a firm, pert backside. He obviously ticked that box because her gaze then swept him over from top to bottom. She was now checking out whether he'd be taller than her, even in heels, and whether he worked out. He ticked those boxes, too. He saw her lips curve into a coy, but most certainly interested smile. He had her attention. There was one box that had yet to be ticked though; the one thing that every woman in the world went gaga for. He simply waited as she sidled up beside him and smiled at the barman, biding her time. They'd get there soon enough. The barman looked at her expectantly, but her attention was elsewhere. Finally she turned her head and stared directly at him. Bingo.

He raised his brilliant blue eyes to hers and blinked slowly, letting his thumb caress the curved glass of his cocktail. It took several moments before she could tear her eyes away from his long enough to notice his drink of choice. Then she smiled and the balance of control tipped.

'Nice drink,' she said, trying, rather miserably, to hide her amused smirk.

'I'm glad you think so,' he said, sliding it smoothly across the bar counter until it sat directly in front of her. 'I bought it for you.' The two black straws and a bright red umbrella that sat in the glass trembled.

Directing his gaze back towards the barman, he ordered a margarita for himself. As the barman busied himself with his new task, stealing sly glances at Violetta whenever he thought he could get away with it, she appeared at a complete loss for words. Staring rather stupidly at the drink in front of her, realising she had been neatly cornered into accepting his offering, she was trying to think of a way to extricate herself from the situation, even though she actually wanted to be there, and what was more, wanted to follow the evening through to a very satisfying conclusion. He knew this for a fact. Being able to read minds was such good fun.

'You need to suck it, to derive much benefit from it,' he commented absently, keeping a perfectly straight face.

Violetta found her voice rather quickly after that, as he suspected she might.

'Gee thanks, Einstein. Are you always this slick with the ladies?' She hopped up elegantly upon a shiny chrome barstool and propped both elbows on the counter. Ah, a stance of power. This he understood. She was trying to tell him to back off with her body language but her eyes were saying something else entirely. Who was it that said eyes were the windows to one's soul? It must have been someone with a moustache and a beard, no doubt, but in any case they might have been on to something.

'No, I'm usually much slicker, but I have a feeling you'd find idle pleasantries rather boring. Isn't that so, princess? Why waste time on such trivial frivolities when we could quickly progress to far more interesting things?'

He got a glare for his troubles, which was so much the better. He was beginning to annoy her and get under her skin. That was exactly where he wanted to be. Scrap that, he wanted to be inside her skin, preferably thrusting away at a rate of knots.

She ignored his loaded question. 'Why did you pick a Pina Colada for me?' It was a safer subject, she wrongly thought.

'For several reasons. It's a long drink, so it should keep you occupied for at least ten minutes, it looks deliciously virginal even though it has quite a kick, and finally, because it's sweet, frothy and doesn't look particularly... intelligent,' he finally answered.

Violetta's jaw worked itself up and down, but no sound came out. It took a few moments before she managed to get over her astonishment at his statement and recover her composure. She finally managed to speak, several seconds after his attack. 'Do you always insult women whom you're trying to chat-up?'

'Now where on earth did you get that idea from? I bought you the drink so you could drink it, and keep quiet, thus allowing me to drink mine in peace. Now if you'd be so gracious, drink the thing and go sit somewhere else.'

Violetta gave him a searing glare of annoyance, which backfired on her rapidly as she found herself trapped between his two mesmerising irises. Giving a growl of disgust at his behaviour and managing to tear her gaze away with more effort than should have been necessary, she relaxed into her barstool. What was most maddening, was the fact that had she not been ordered to sit elsewhere, she would have. Now, if she wanted to stand her ground, she would have to endure his company for the length of her cocktail. Had it been anything other than a Pina Colada she would have dumped the contents over his head, but he had unwittingly picked her favourite drink - which was even more exasperating. Apparently, it was not going to be her evening.

Picking up the cool glass and wrapping her fingers carefully around the wet surface, she stirred the contents with her straw and watched as the cubes of ice gently danced around one another. Taking a long, slow and comforting swallow of the fragrant liquid, she beckoned the barman over, who immediately raced forward to do her bidding. He hadn't really taken his eyes off her since she'd sat down. His smiling, friendly face was somewhat reassuring although Violetta wouldn't have trusted him with her honour, any more than Mr Unsociable in the corner.

'Is he normally this miserable?' It was a conspiratorial whisper, but she made sure it was just loud enough that the irritating man would be able to hear it.

The barman thoughtfully rubbed his tanned, bald head and grinned at her. 'No. Normally he's much worse, ma'am. I think he likes you.' There was a knowing wink. The barman did not lower his voice as Violetta had done, but if the strange man overheard their conversation he made no show of the fact.

'So what's his problem?'

The barman twisted his lips sympathetically and sighed. 'He's had a few deaths in the family. He needs cheering up, I think.' Placing a small terracotta bowl of spiced peanuts on the counter next to her, and making a great show of polishing an already immaculately sparkling wine glass, he made it clear that he had no wish to continue the conversation. Violetta consoled herself by trying to place his accent, which could have been Malaysian or something similar, and for a moment she couldn't remember for the life of her why she would be so far away from home. Her head felt oddly fuzzy and disjointed. The disturbing thought left her mind almost as soon it had entered, and she felt compelled to take another soothing sip of her cocktail.

'He needs drowning, more like,' she said, but it was barely a murmur under her breath.

The dark-haired stranger pulled a circle of lime from the side of his salted martini glass and proceeded to eat the whole thing, rind and all. Violetta couldn't help but suck in her cheeks and wince.

'Oh my God,' she said aghast, covering her mouth with her hand. 'I bet that tasted disgusting.'

The stranger deigned to give her a slight incline of his head and the response, 'There's only one thing that tastes good these days. Everything else hardly matters.'

Violetta didn't want to ask the question, but he'd popped the idea inside her head and there was no way of stopping it. 'And what, pray tell, is that?'

'Annihilation,' he said, drinking the rest of his margarita in one long, smooth, sensuous gulp, before adding, 'but oblivion would also work, I think.' He straightened himself up, cracked his neck to the side and picked up his blazer, which had been laid casually across the end of the counter. Without a single glance back in her direction the sexy, moody stranger strode out of her life without so much as a 'goodbye'.

Violetta watched his retreating form and tried not to pine after him. What was it with bad boys? What was it about that morose, sulky exterior that left her so intrigued? The butt was good, the figure was slim but filled in all the right places and the eyes, oh those eyes, she could have swam in them forever. There went one troubled soul. She was almost tempted to go after him, but his sharply sarcastic tongue would probably be most unappreciative of her grand gesture.

Squirming about in her seat for several seconds, finally she couldn't resist asking, 'Where's he off to?'

After several moments of silence she thought the barman had decided to ignore her, but finally he pursed his lips and sighed. 'He's suicidal, Ma'am. He's lost everyone he's ever been close to. You'd do well to move on and forget him.'

After inquiring whether she'd like another drink and finding the answer to be 'no', he disappeared into the back room without further comment. This enabled Violetta to shoot out of the bar, faster than a German tourist reserving his sun-lounger for the day, to search for the manic-depressive who could obviously only be saved by her.

There was no one around of course. The wooden walkway she found herself on had been lit up with bright candle lanterns, and tiny fairy-lights glittered from above. They had been suspended on a leafy trellis littered with hibiscus plants. On either side of the large planks she stood on there was nothing but water, a very large expanse of water, as it happened. They were in a hotel which appeared to have been placed in the middle of the ocean.

As soon as she realised there was nothing but water wherever she looked, Violetta almost ran back to the bar for comfort. She felt oddly off-balance and unsettled. Looking down the row of planks as far as the eye could see revealed little more than a vast array of twinkling, flickering amber lights, but she guessed the walkway probably ended somewhere sensible and not in the middle of the big watery waste that was, for tonight at least, her home.

Placing one foot in front of the other, she navigated the wooden slats with care. High-heeled sandals had been a silly choice of footwear for a midnight stroll on what appeared to be a path little better constructed than a rope bridge, but she'd made up her mind to search for the stranger and it would be fair to say she was a stubborn-minded individual. So she concentrated on moving forward, very carefully, and let her eyes become accustomed to the dark. There was little in the way of sounds to be heard. A couple of splashes from a few over-exuberant fish, but other than that the world had gone to sleep. She looked for a watch, but found her left wrist naked. How strange. She never went anywhere without one. Trying to analyse the thought and make sense of it, she found no answers forthcoming. What was wrong with her this evening? Her brain didn't want to focus, that was for sure. It was becoming so frustrating that she wanted to shake herself.

In the distance she began to make out the shape of several small villas, each rearing out of water by the addition of four wooden columns. They looked like long-limbed wading birds, rising majestically out of the deep blue. Suddenly there was a flash of movement and she caught a glimpse of silver reflected on the water. It made her jump and in the next moment she was falling.

She'd taken a miss-step and her sandaled foot had managed to wedge itself in one of the gaps along the walkway. A shocked gasp left her lips as her body buckled forward and prepared to meet several slabs of timber. Her arms shot out instinctively to soften her fall, but in the end they found themselves redundant. The stranger appeared out of nowhere and his arms snaked around her, pulling her smartly upright. He managed to dislodge her foot out of the two planks it had become trapped in, and without a single word being spoken, he slung her up over his shoulder and carried her down the remaining pathway until it widened out in front of a small enclosure of wooden huts.

Violetta was too shocked to do little but stare agape at his backside. Being slung upside down was not something which happened to her very often. She was a tall woman and most men usually kept their distance, finding her a little intimidating. Thinking she should be pummelling her hands upon his back and demanding that he right her this instance, he must have read her mind for she found herself once again back on her feet, the landing brutal.

'Nice ass,' she commented, when her teeth had recovered from their vicious snap together, and she gave him a furious stare through shuttered lashes.

'Nice panties,' he countered, in that awful, deep, sexy voice that did funny things to her body, and then he tilted his head and looked sideways at her.

Violetta looked down to discover that the ends of her dress had become entangled in her stocking top, displaying a fair amount of flesh and a sizeable portion of her tan bikini panties. Growling, her face flooding with heat, she managed to tear the offending garment back down, but she'd already seen his smile and her body had almost frozen. It was the wide smile of a predator. The smile of a man who knew what he wanted and how to have it expertly delivered in his lap. She felt her heartbeat stutter and she wanted to run. Every nerve-ending screamed for flight and she would have given in to them had the stranger not abruptly turned his back on her and sat down on the edge of the decking. She had been dismissed without a word for the second time that evening and the feeling was not a warm and fuzzy one.

Deciding to head straight back to the bar and somehow get her butt the hell out of this place, her eyes strayed down to his hand, which was playing with something. Long and silver, it must have been what she'd spied reflected upon the water, and it could only be one thing. He flipped it over and over in dexterous fingers, and the knife appeared to come alive in his hands - a living, breathing entity.

Violetta had already begun to turn her body around in order to stalk back to safety, but the sight of the knife stopped her. He was a human being, albeit an extremely unpleasant one, and he was obviously in pain. Whilst she had no idea if he really intended to kill himself, she could hardly leave him here, like this. The man needed help.

'Do you want to talk?'

'I think we already covered that at the bar.' The stranger didn't even turn around to glance at her.

She knew she should have just walked straight back the way she came as his surly remark hit home, but like a moth drawn to a decidedly enticing flame she couldn't help but try one last time. 'What do you want?'

'I want to fuck the hell out of you.'

Violetta was not a particularly quiet woman, but he'd thrown her a massive curve ball and it seemed she'd swallowed the thing. It took her several seconds before she could suck in air.

'What did you say?' Her voice was incredulous.

'If you want a repeat performance, you have to beg. That goes for the sentence and the sex.' He kicked off his shoes, letting them sail away in the water beneath him. He then removed his black blazer and let it go the same way.

'You're mad,' she whispered, her feet already backing up behind her. At least one part of her body was sensible, Violetta thought.

There was a sharp thud and she watched as he buried the small knife he'd been playing with deep into the timber decking. There was a dull twang as the thing vibrated rapidly at the impact and then silence resumed. She bit her lip and wondered absently why she was not running away as fast as her legs would carry her, but it was already too late. In the next instance he was up on his feet and striding purposefully towards her. His fingers were already unbuttoning his shirt, revealing tempting glimpses of the tantalisingly hard flesh beneath and she felt her feet automatically backing up until they reached the edge of the planks.

'There's nowhere else to go, Violetta,' he drawled, as he came within a hairbreadth's length of touching her. He brought his fingertip underneath her chin and tilted her face upwards to meet his.

'How do you know my name?' She looked up at him, and there was a mixture of angst and desire in her gaze. It was difficult to know which was stronger. One thing was for certain, he seemed to have all the right cards in his hand and she wanted to know why.

'That's the least of your worries, precious. What you should be asking is: "How do I know every move you're going to make, seconds before you do?" The flat of his hand reached down to slap her left knee away, the one that had been about try and find a soft spot around his groin area. The knee landed back on the wooden deck with a considerable thump and she felt herself wobble precariously.

'How in the hell...?' Her shocked words left her lips and were instantly cut off as she felt herself falling backwards. Her hands floundered helplessly at his naked chest, but there was nothing she could grab onto for purchase and as her heel skidded and splintered across the deck there was the sinking feeling she was way past the point of no return. Preparing to take a deep splosh in the uninviting, wet and salty stuff, she closed her eyes and braced herself for impact.

Amazingly enough, she didn't end up going for a midnight swim. The impact still happened, but the splosh did not. Mr Grumpy had managed to save the day by encompassing two tight arms around her body and somehow managing to retain his balance with her heavy weight in his arms.

'You're not that heavy,' he mind-blowingly said, before bringing her face up to meet his.

She hadn't said that last thought out loud, surely? But if she hadn't, that would mean the man could read... No. Violetta refused to consider the possibility. She knew of only one creature that could read minds and that would make him a...

41

'Vampire.' He poured the single word into her lips with sultry intent and then all further thought left her. He took her with a fierce, all-consuming hunger and damned if he didn't recreate the same reciprocal need in her. His lips were soft and he locked them cleverly around hers, while his fingers threaded their way through her hair. He gave gentle tugs with his hand to position her just where he wanted her, and the man was good. Here was a beast who knew exactly what he was doing and how to use each and every little action to the best advantage. A hand came up to caress the soft spot directly under her jawline and as he pressed his chest into her body she wanted to melt. That was a lie. She'd already melted and was little more than a puddle of liquid in his arms. The vamp had skills. His finger was tracing a light path over the top of her lips and she already yearned for the taste of his tongue, thrusting against hers. To encourage and hasten the proceedings she gently coaxed herself into his mouth and hoped he'd get the message.

'Such a greedy little thing, aren't you? And here I was thinking you'd put up a fight, me being one of the dreaded un-dead and all.'

Violetta didn't want to let that comment inside her head because she was really having far too much fun, half out of her mind with lust. It fluttered about a bit and begged for attention, but she did her best to ignore it. It was relatively easy as soon as his tongue was brought into play and, oh dear God, Master seducer didn't even begin to describe him. There was nothing the man couldn't do. One hand cupped the heat of her sex while his teeth grazed and nibbled at her lips. His tongue battled hers for supremacy, and she was more than glad to offer her submission. He had her breathing hard in seconds and her eyes were nearly black with desire. Everything began to wobble and shake, and it was almost as if all her dreams were about to come true at once. A tall, dark, brooding stranger had just saved her from imminent death and was now about to have his wicked way with her. Talk about schoolgirl fantasy. It was sublime. Letting her body relax into the strong arms she wound her hands around his neck and kissed him with an end-of-the-world-is-nigh, apocalyptic passion.

When he tore his lips away from hers she gave him a guttural moan of protest at the loss of contact, but he was quick to return, laving a wet path along her neck with his tongue. Then she felt two sharp teeth elongating rapidly and steering themselves towards her jugular, scraping against her delicate skin. She tried to rear up from his grasp in sudden panic, but the tight hold he had on her body made any movement virtually impossible.

'Holy hell, you were just about to bite me!' The accusation was an angry, shrill one. For some reason she knew she could not be bitten. It was an important detail, but her brain did not offer up any more clues. Alas, he did not seem in the least bit bothered by her protests and his teeth continued their abrasive journey up and down the soft skin just below her ear. When she tugged his hair sharply, to let him know she meant business, he finally raised his head, before clucking his tongue in annoyance.

'Yes, I believe we have already ascertained that I'm a vampire. That's what vampires do. They find a suitable neck, grow a set of fangs and then they...'

'I'm familiar with the mechanics, thank you very much,' she said through gritted teeth, 'I'm a huntress!' There it was. That's what was so important. She killed vampires. Oh good lord.

He pouted for a second. 'Can't you just forget about killing things for a minute and let me finish the job in hand? We're still in a rather delicate position here.'

He wasn't joking. The man still held her in the deep dip he had caught her in. She was bent double and half her body was currently suspended over the ocean, head first. As lovely as he was, the idea of being bitten by a vampire was not tempting and would be a rather permanent lifestyle change in her case. The consequences were a little too high to be considered. 'No, you can't bite me. Put me down.' Her voice was firm and authoritative, but the stranger took no notice. Once again his lips were back on hers and she was drowning without the aid of an ocean. Up to her neck in a thirst for flesh that could not be quenched with anything less than bodily fluids, she knew it would be far too easy to get lost in him.

Get him off you, the voice of reason called, and quick, before he does all of those terrible, wonderful things you've heard so much about. The trouble was that the rest of her body did not want to listen or take the sensible option. Her conscience had been left somewhere far, far away on dry land and that was just peachy as far as she was concerned. Or it was until his lips began nuzzling at her neck once more, and his teeth gave her a vicious nip which made her cry out. Damn. Where was a stake when you needed one?

'Get off me. We can't do this. Christ, I should be looking for ways to kill you and you should be running. I'm the best there is.'

His free hand reached up towards her breast, gave it a modest squeeze and then he let his thumb rove gently over her nipple. He raised his mouth from her neck to reply, 'I've also been told that, but it wasn't in relation to killing people and the clientele were ninety-nine percent female. Very happy females, as I recall. Why don't you let yourself go for a change, chérie, and see where the moment takes you. His hand squeezed harder, cleverly manipulating the soft mound of flesh before his fingers managed to tweak her nipple through the sheer fabric of the camisole beneath. He once again pressed his fangs to her neck, and this time he applied some pressure.

'Don't touch me. Get off me you bastard!' She began to struggle in earnest, although she didn't manage to release one single limb from his all-encompassing embrace. But the words did manage to get through to him, as he removed his teeth from her jawline and gave her a look of irritation.

'Well, as you've asked so nicely, I suppose I must consider your request,' he sighed. He appeared to give the matter some thought and she could feel her heart doing cartwheels beneath his chest. There was no way she could be bitten. Please, please, she begged, let this be a vamp with a semblance of morality.

'Fine, fine.' He stretched his neck first to the left and then to the right, where a subtle cracking noise could be heard. Violetta winced inwardly. There was then a calculated pause before he said, 'Never say that we vampires are not gentlemen. We can overcome our basest desires in order to please a woman any day of the week. You have asked to be let go, and so you shall be.'

Violetta barely heard the last word he had uttered for she was falling. Into the goddamned ocean! When she had asked to be released she expected to be put down on terra firma. A silent scream bubbled in her throat. It had no time to be let loose for the water was rushing up to greet her and panic was already beginning to consume her. Although she had many great talents in the world, swimming was not one of them. Being bitten now seemed like the much more preferable option when faced with a certain death situation, and then there was no more thought, for she plunged into the water and sank to the bottom of the sea.

Violetta's thoughts came tumbling back down around her as soon as she was immersed in the deep black pool of the ocean. The thing that had surprised her most about the fall was that the water was warm. Not just mildly, pleasantly tepid, but bathwater, beautifully-hot warm. Where in the world were they? It was somewhere close to the equator, at any rate. As her hair writhed all around her in suffocating waves, she tried to dash it out of her face with her hands. To what ends she hoped to achieve was anybody's guess, for there was little to see anywhere around her in the dead of night. The world began to revolve in slow motion as her body sunk silently downward, but then things sped up with startling speed.

When she finally stopped falling everything seemed to operate in reverse. It was almost as if the ocean had rejected her and wanted to spit her out, for now she was shooting back upwards and a moment of hope began to take root in her brain. Maybe she'd manage to get to the surface, maybe she'd be able to float to one of the thick timber poles beneath the small huts, and maybe she'd somehow find a way to get back up and into the small cluster of villas without dying. It was a lot of maybes, though, and she didn't really fancy her chances. Her breath was compressing tightly in her chest, her lungs felt like they were about to explode and all she could see was a never-ending, aquatic graveyard of blue-black darkness. She wanted to scream, but there was nowhere for it to go. Surely the vamp wouldn't leave her here to die? But then, that's what vamps were good at, wasn't it? Certain death, blood, suffering and all that...

As her head burst up through the surface of the waves she opened her mouth and took in a great gulp of much needed air, along with a sizeable portion of salt water, which had her spluttering and coughing. Spying her antagonist, standing still as a sentry on the jetty above, she cried out towards him in a blind panic, 'I can't swim!' As her arms splashed and flopped against the waves in helpless circles, having no clue what to do with themselves, she looked up at him pleadingly.

'Can you not?' His voice carried loudly over the waves and she had no problem hearing his next acerbic comment. 'Then I suspect it's a rather unfortunate phenomenon finding yourself in the middle of the ocean.'

Violetta's head went under the water once more, and she had to flap around frantically to bring her head back to the surface. 'Help me!' Her cries were frantic, her tone pleading.

He didn't seem at all concerned with her plight, standing tall against the skyline, his back illuminated by the soft yellow lights of the villas beyond. To make sure he well-and-truly got the urgency of her message she began screaming it over and over until she heard his voice again.

'Look,' he said testily, 'I want to help, really I do, but you've asked me not to touch you. So, keeping that in mind, a rescue is going to be a little bit difficult. On the plus side your unfortunate demise might restore peace and sanity to my world, so be a good girl and go quietly.'

There was lots of shrieking, lots of sploshing and a frustrated roar before Violetta managed to get her next sentence out. 'What do you want?'

'Your soul,' came the unerring reply, 'but I'll settle for a good fuck, as I think I've mentioned. No kicking or screaming. You do everything I say. We have a deal?'

'Yes.' Violetta had just managed to swallow yet another mouthful of salt water and was eager to agree to just about any term he had, bar one. 'Anything you like, but no biting.' The 'ng' sound came out wrong, mostly uttered underneath the water in bubbles, but she guessed he'd get the message.

'I hardly think you're in any position to barter, are you, my dear?'

Lots of sounds greeted him in response, mostly splashes and gurgling, but the words 'rather' and 'die' were most definitely mentioned.

'Do you want to test that theory?' It was a casual question, but then she went under the deep blue for the longest time and he'd just about primed himself to jump in, before she managed to get to the surface in time.

There was a frantic gasp for air before her final terms were spoken. 'No biting.'

'Fine. We have a deal,' he said resignedly. He had no idea he could be so noble. It was an almost painful thought. He contemplated it meditatively and couldn't help but wonder if he was losing his touch in his old age.

Violetta, still floundering around madly, watched his unmoving body for several painful moments and had an awful suspicion that he might have changed his mind.

'Well? Are you going to rescue me or not?' Her voice was more than a little agitated now, pretty much like the rest of her body, which was rolling about in the waves like a set of die in a Las Vegas gambling den.

He immediately snapped out of his reverie. 'There is such impatience inside you, for one so young. Of course I'm coming to rescue you; why do you think I removed my blazer and shoes?' With that he took an elegant dive off the wooden jetty that a dolphin would have been proud of, and hit the water at a perfect forty-five degree angle. Then he disappeared.

Violetta was unsure what made her more nervous; the possibility of drowning or the possibility of being attacked by an underwater vampire who was no less dangerous than a shark. She knew he didn't need to breathe, so there was little chance she'd see his head above water before he reached her. In his world air was about as precious as a grain of sand. Lucky for him, she thought, swallowing yet another mouthful of briny liquid as she tried desperately to stay afloat. Looking down upon the surface of the ocean, trying to see past the gentle waves, she looked for signs of movement, but of course there was nothing. Vamps moved with remarkable agility and speed. This meant she wouldn't see him until he was nearly in front of her, but she wondered if he'd get to her in time. She was exhausted, her arms felt heavy and her body could have been a lead weight, dragging her down at every opportunity. Fight as she might to stay afloat, going under was happening all too frequently and she didn't know whether she'd have the energy to pull herself back up next time. Plunging under the waves for the umpteenth time she felt her dress billowing out all around her and a sense of total desolation and despair. She didn't trust the vamp in the slightest. He might, even now, be watching from the sidelines, waiting for her to drown in a pool of her own misery, so he could have an easy late night snack. It wasn't as if he'd be shedding any tears if she'd breathed her last breath. Inhaling water into her lungs, her eyes frantically darted to and fro, hoping to catch a glimpse of something, anything, before all conscious thought left her. As her eyes began to see black spots slowly spreading across her field of vision and her eyelids drooped, she wondered if he would have managed to swim a bit quicker had she offered to be bitten...

Suddenly there was an almighty force beneath her body and she felt herself shooting upwards, breaking through water's edge and then falling back down into a pair of sturdy arms. She was then roughly thrown over his shoulder, and he used the flat of his hand against her back to help her cough up the remnants of the ocean deep. It was not a particularly pleasant experience. When she'd finally managed to give back most of the fluid she'd stolen he twisted her around in his arms and sighed.

'If there was a wet T-shirt competition in these parts tonight, you'd win by a mile.'

Violetta, furious after her near-death experience, flared a pair of violent, violet eyes his way before her hand reached up to slap him. He simply caught it, imprisoned it and smiled. 'You humans are so frustrating,' he sighed, reaching up to caress the tip of a nipple, clearly outlined by the soaked, see-through material of her dress. 'You know I'm a killer, you know I'm dangerous and yet, still, you act in a totally deranged manner after I've taken the trouble to come and rescue you. If you want to die so badly, be my guest.' He abruptly released his hold on her and her body instantly began to sink.

Violetta screeched and flapped about, her arms lashing out to find some kind of purchase on his body before she went under yet again. 'I'm sorry,' she sobbed. 'I'm sorry. I'll play by your rules. Just get me out of here.' Her hands managed to find their way around his neck and she clung onto his body for dear life.

'Hmm,' he said, tipping his face down to meet hers and letting his dark gaze do its worst. 'So, let me reiterate our deal, to avoid confusion. We're going to have sex and you're going to do everything I say. The "everything I say" part is rather important. We clear?'

'You were playing nicely before?' At her caustic words he gave her a raised eyebrow and began to push her away from him.

'We're clear, we're clear! Everything you say. No kicking or screaming. I remember.' Her arms had taken on an almost limpet-like quality around his shoulders and she buried her face in his neck. 'No biting though, please,' her voice was small and resigned against his chest.

'That was the agreement,' he nodded. Picking her up once again, cradling her backside in his arms, he watched as her breasts moved and swayed with the current. He observed her for at least a full, silent minute before he issued his first command.

'Touch yourself for me.'

Violetta saw where his gaze had stopped and she knew exactly what he wanted from her, but had absolutely no idea how to go about it. 'I don't know what you mean,' she whispered, and then added in a panic, 'but I'm willing to do it, if you explain. Touch myself, how?'

Martinet sighed and rolled his eyes. Virgins were one moment delightful, and in the next, paradoxically, a pain in the ass. 'Your breasts, darling; I want you to touch them for me. I don't mind if you knead them, stroke them, rub them or pull at them - just do what feels nice. I want you to pleasure yourself for me.'

The girl looked at her hands rather helplessly for a minute and bit her lip. It wasn't so much that she didn't know where to place her hands, or even how to begin, the issue was that he was watching her. He waited for the inevitable plea and it wasn't long in coming.

'Couldn't you just close your eyes? Or perhaps look in the other direction? I don't feel comfortable...' She yelped. He'd relaxed his tight hold on her, which meant her body was sinking back into the water.

'Now where would the fun be in that? The whole point of this exercise is that I become aroused watching you play with yourself. I want to see those eyelashes flutter, I want to hear you moan in heat, but most of all, I want to watch for that special moment when you forget I'm even here.' He smiled cynically, 'Though I'll most probably remind you, shortly after.' He whipped his hands out from underneath her and let her splash around for a bit. She was even more stubborn than he'd given her credit for, or completely stupid. He wasn't quite sure which.

'OK, OK!' Her hands were quick to grasp both her breasts, in compliance with his wishes, and he rewarded her with the comforting presence of his hands.

'The next time you fail to obey my order immediately I'm walking and I'm not coming back.' The biting words rang out loudly and echoed in her head. If Violetta was in any doubt to the sincerity of them, one glance at his humourless face told her all she needed to know. The man was deadly serious. Well, what did she expect? It wasn't as if he had a conscience. He was a deranged, monstrous, sexy-as-hell, drop-dead-gorgeous blood-sucker and she'd do well to follow his instruction to the letter and run whenever an opportunity presented itself. For now, she was going to do everything he said. It helped that a hundred-weight of endorphins had now started to rattle through her body at breakneck pace and all she wanted was for the beast to get his hands on her and show her a good time. She'd heard so much about the act of lovemaking, and had yet to put any of it into practise. Now that she had no choice but to follow his every instruction, the embarrassment of being watched left her, to a degree, and she began to explore her body as instructed.

Long fingers stretched out and fanned over the generous expanse of her cleavage, giving the twin mounds of protruding flesh little more than a gentle sweep of her fingertips. Violetta had never thought about touching her body before and was surprised to discover that even a gentle touch was actually quite pleasant. Ignoring the dark, brooding, sexy vampire, who was now eye-balling her wet dress and the many curves it revealed from head to toe, she let her fingernails scrape across her delicate flesh, delving inside the wet folds of material that flopped all around her. When they caught the underside of her breasts she bit her lip and inhaled deeply.

It wasn't long before she was experimenting with different touches. Her thumbs applied a little pressure to her outer curves and then she allowed them to massage the soft skin in small concentric strokes, pressing harder and harder until it achieved the desired result - a soft groan of pleasure. If she'd known how much fun this would be she'd have done it years ago.

'You've only just begun, princess. When you progress to the nipple you'll find out what you've really been missing.' He wore a large smirk across his face as he greedily took in her body and hands, but at that moment in time she couldn't have cared less. With each soft stroke she felt herself relaxing into the soothing heat of the water and the large hands that cushioned her backside and wrapped around her neck. The feeling that washed through her was one of safety and protection, although she knew all too well how insane that was. The thought fizzled out as soon as it formed, almost as if someone had whipped it out of her brain. Surely not. That couldn't be possible, could it? Her hands faltered in their task.

'I want to see those nipples hard, chérie. I want to admire them poking through the wet fabric of your dress, proudly stating their intentions. They need to beg to be taken. Get them as hard as you can, Vi, so the feel of my hot tongue and lips against them will be almost painful, for I mean to show you just how sensitive those delicious nubs can be.' He brought his lips to the shell of her ear and began to nibble at her lobe. Wondering how she could concentrate on anything with his warm breath tickling her neck, somehow, she managed to obey. His voice, dark, sinister and dangerous as hell, had a tone that compelled her to follow and hang off his every word. She was in no mood to fight its insidious pull, for her body was in heat. Finger and thumb had now paired together in a pincer grip and she was lightly pulling at her left nipple. The feeling was exquisite. Her body arched up, out of the water, and his two hands had to catch her as she swiftly returned. Little tendrils of electric pleasure flowed through her as she repeated her actions over and over, alternating between both breasts until she decided to get greedy. Playing with them both at once, but this time letting her fingertips tug at the delicate teats more sharply, she revelled in the fierce pressure and gasped at what the additional stimulation did to her. Arousal flowed through her, bursting out of every pore, driving her insane with the need to move, squirm and undulate her body. It wanted something, she had no idea what, but there was definitely something her fingers were seeking. They moved faster, tugged harder and squeezed her flesh almost painfully in their quest for that elusive, indefinable something. What was it she now craved with an almost ethereal passion? Her hands were not going to stop until she discovered the answers to her questions...

'Ah, but that's where you are wrong, chérie.' His voice came out of nowhere and made her jump. Her hands dropped to her sides and her heartrate accelerated painfully for a minute. Making an irritated mewl of protest, annoyed that he had disturbed her quest for pleasure, she took a moment to realise that he had been correct in his predictions. She had completely forgotten he was there. Her cheeks flooded with colour at the thought, but it didn't stop her hands continuing their explorations.

'Uh, uh, uh.' The safety of his arms beneath her was removed and she quickly whipped her hands out to the side and began to splash about for all she was worth.

'Lie flat. Arms out to your sides, legs splayed wide. If you keep that position you'll float. Obey or face the consequences, princess.' He kept a single hand beneath her, to allow her to comply with his wishes, and his hypnotic blue eyes bored into hers. She didn't have the strength to resist them. Automatically following his commands, her body had almost taken on a life of its own. Legs spread open wide and arms were thrown out to the side, as she wondered what on earth she was doing. He was quick to remove his hand as she assumed his required pose, and for a moment she felt nothing but agonised panic, but amazingly, she remained above water.

'Make sure those hands stay where they are. If you feel your head slipping under the water just flap them about a bit, like this.' He demonstrated what he meant by using his own two arms, stretching them out to his sides and moving them forward and back in a gentle sweeping motion. She nodded her understanding. 'Now that you've done all the hard work and aroused yourself, rather beautifully I might add, you're all mine. I can do whatever I like to that body of yours and there isn't a thing you can do about it, because if you deviate from that position you're holding you'll sink, and I believe I've already mentioned I won't be rescuing you. However, if you allow me a little fun, then I'll get you back to dry land shortly. For now, just buckle up and enjoy the ride.' He winked at her, and even that tiny, harmless little action had her body trembling with excitement. What was the beast going to do to her? Unsure whether to be scared or deliriously pleased at the thought of him having his wicked way with her, she could do nothing but wait expectantly for his next move and unfortunately, he was in no hurry.

'Orgasms are usually better when they're delayed. It's called edging. If I bring you to the point of near-climax and stop just as you're peering over the cliff to the pathway of gratification, that will rev up your libido somewhat. If I do it several times I'll have you sobbing and begging for mercy. That should mean that when you finally achieve your goal you'll feel as if your whole body is imploding, from the inside out. Fortunately for you, I'm one of these people who has to do everything properly. Actually, that may be unfortunately for you, depending on your latter tolerance for pain, but we'll talk about that later. I'm jumping ahead of myself.'

Violetta's mind tried to process the sounds coming out of his mouth, but most of it flew in one ear to be immediately ejected by the other. There was a good reason for her lack of concentration. Her vampire had just positioned his body between her legs and his hands were making their way underneath her sodden dress and slowly up her legs. Her immediate reaction was to close her legs and try her best to slap him out of the way. It didn't matter that they'd agreed to have sex, actually doing it and having his hands on her was another matter entirely. As her legs began to close, though, her body began to sink.

'Hold that stance, darling, or you'll be diving to the bottom of the ocean in short order.' This time she did hear his words, and when she felt her body begin to dip haphazardly in the middle, her bottom pulling the rest of her downwards, she decided it would be sensible to do exactly as he said for the time being. Her legs thrust outward once more and her arms stayed proudly perpendicular to her body. He had rendered her helpless in one easy move and there wasn't a thing she could do about it. She would have to endure whatever it was he was about to throw at her. It couldn't be half as bad as drowning, could it? As his hands once again reached under her skirt and slowly crept upward she began to wonder.

'I don't even know your name,' she said, in a little voice that couldn't possibly have been hers, sounding raspy and breathless.

'Michel,' he offered amiably enough, before adding, 'but you may call me God.'

'Ha, ha, very funny,' she whispered, but once again her voice sounded wrong, for his hands had found the innermost tips of her thighs and were caressing the edges of her satin panties. It took all the strength she possessed to remember to hold her position and not squirm away from his tormenting fingers.

'Oh, believe you me, you will be calling me God before the night is out, and that's a promise.' He cast his gaze along her body, from the tips of her toes to the interesting glare that turned down the corners of her mouth and brightened the gleam of her shimmering violet eyes. The effect was quite breathtaking, and had he been a creature that needed to breathe he would surely have stolen every wisp of air inside him.

'You have no idea how beautiful you look like that, you know. All soft curves and beautifully outlined contours. Your dress looks like it's been spray-painted on and with your nipples poking out like little homing beacons for my mouth, well, it does funny things to my insides, precious.' The glare deepened and he could see her body twitching, itching to move and run away from him as fast as her legs would carry her. Alas, that wouldn't be an option for her any time soon. She was such an ungrateful thing, he thought. Most women would happily die for his attention, and to be fair, plenty had when he'd been nothing more than a mere fledgling. She should be grateful he had a measure of control these days.

His fingers moved inside the lace hem of her panties and ran delicately along the textured surface. He approved of her soggy wet panties and the soaking wet dress, but had to wonder what else might be wet for him. Although this was his vision and he controlled things to a certain extent, for the time being her level of arousal was her own. If he had to play around inside her head to achieve his desired result, he would, but he hoped that wouldn't be necessary. As his fingers tangled in a thatch of tight curly hair, he took a moment to consider whether his huntress was a natural redhead. All would be revealed shortly, but for now he was going to have a little bet with himself. He was almost certain that she was. Burrowing his hand inside the front of her panties and grasping a handful of her hair, he gave it a mild tug. She let out a gasp, but did little more than flap her hands anxiously in protest. There wasn't a lot else she could do, which was just as well, because he decided to give her a few more tugs just to pull her chain. He was thoroughly enjoying himself this evening and considering how miserable he'd been these past couple of years, he decided he deserved a little pick-me-up in the form of her deliciously ripe, untrained body. Oh, the things he could do with her.

Pressing his body into her crotch, letting her feel the thick length of his cock as it rubbed against the entrance to her sex, he watched as her eyes widened and winked at her. 'It's impressive, isn't it? Don't worry, you'll be getting your fair share of that later. One of the benefits of being a vampire is that when you go through the change, everything improves slightly. In my case, I went from python to anaconda.

'How nice for you,' Violetta murmured, in a strangled kind of whisper.

'Not half as nice as it's going to be for you,' he said with a wicked smile. 'We'll need to get you wet enough to accommodate me first, and that's going to require a little bit of work on my part, but don't you worry about a thing. You can just lie back and take it easy, sweetheart.' Her frustrated scream and vigorous arm waving did nothing to cool his ardour. He was already pushing her panties aside, so that the clever fingers of his right hand could work her clit, while the talented fingers of his left could thrust away happily inside her. His feet would have to paddle madly to stay afloat, but that wasn't going to be hard graft for a being such as himself.

She was wet, and mad, and really, really magnificently tight. Beginning with a single digit he spread a little of her own lubricant generously around her perineum, the area that was above water in any case. It was a blessing she was soaked because he didn't feel particularly patient this evening. One dextrous finger became two and he used them in tandem to stretch her wide open. Using long, gentle thrusts which would relax and torment her, he scrutinised her face carefully. The glare slowly disappeared, to be replaced with a look of surprise and, perhaps, disbelief. We haven't even started yet, he thought in amusement. Pumping her over and over with his fingers, he couldn't help but notice she was truly beautiful in each and every response, her body sending little ripples of current this way and that as she trembled and splashed.

Her flapping arms were becoming a little bit more uncoordinated now, and it was only when she began to sink beneath the waves that she remembered to flutter them about frantically. That was when he decided to up the ante a little bit. He was going to give her an early showing of the Martinet Magic Mouth, or the triple 'M' for short. It had a one hundred percent success rate. Having been tested on both males and females in its long and glorious career, it had received not one complaint. It wasn't about to sully its tick sheet tonight, either.

Placing two hands underneath her buttocks and letting his body float to the surface, much the same as hers except the other way around, he used his feet to keep himself buoyant while his head dipped towards the apex of her thighs. He began his gentle torment by blowing a thin stream of bubbles at her sex. Watching her body buck and twist at the sensation, he blew a little harder. By the way she was thrashing about you'd think he was causing her pain, but he knew differently. Next he let his mouth clamp over her panty-covered clit, imparting scorching heat while his hands grabbed her dress and pulled her closer to him. He tongued her thoroughly through the salty wet fabric and watched her squirm. Then he gave her a few tantalisingly slow licks from the top of her clit to the bottom. From the tight grip he had on her thighs he felt her legs wobble and knew he'd hit the right spot.

'I'm going to have great fun edging you to bigger and better orgasmic achievements, and we'll practise every evening until you can successfully withstand at least ten attempts, before going for the prize result. We'll have you an edging queen in no time.' He swept the covering of her panties away with his thumb and then let loose the real power of his mouth. Delivering soft laps, small flicks, a few long sucks and popping her clit back and forth between his lips, he had her mindless and legless in no time at all. The poor chit would have sunk on numerous occasions too, had it not been for the strong grip he had around her waist and the constant movement of his feet.

'Ready to call me God yet?' He brought his head up out of the water, shook his hair to get rid of the excess water and watched as he splattered her body with tiny pearls of water, lit up by nothing more than the wan light of a waxing moon. While they were on the subject of waxing, that hair she had down there would have to go, but he'd issue his demands later. Right now he wanted her limp, panting and breathless.

'You're an asshole.' His princess had the most delicious temper. He wondered if they should work to subdue it or if he would let it have full reign and then show her the consequences of such displays of emotion. They would not be tolerated in the vampire world, and even though he was not yet positive he would change her, the odds of it happening were beginning to look ever more favourable.

He blinked at her several times and then pressed his index finger sharply against her sphincter. He gave her a lengthy sigh to make sure she sensed his displeasure at her curt comment. 'No, darling, this is an asshole and I intend to do big things with it later. That will take some practise though, so you can breathe easy for the time being.' A hand forked through his hair to bring the dark mass away from his brow, and his face dipped below the surface of the water once more, seeking the sweet spot of her body, which tasted far better than any human food ever had.

He suckled and tongued. Flicked, forked, pulsated and tickled, and just as her face creased up tightly with the painful effort of holding her orgasm back, he stopped. He withdrew his tongue, licked his lips and tilted his head towards her with the biggest smile on his face.

'You...' her voice was tight and venomous. It was clear she was in pain, the pleasurable kind at least. He cut her off before the woman earned a spanking her bottom couldn't yet cash.

'You call me an asshole again and I'll stretch this tight little hole of yours to proportions you would not believe possible.' Withdrawing his fingers from her pussy he pressed his lubricated fingers against the smaller, puckered hole that was a touch further down and pressed for entry.

'No, no, please God, no,' she whimpered, her body thrashing and bucking at the contact as she sank into the wet wasteland of ripples below her.

He raised an eyebrow. 'I told you you'd be calling me God before the night was out, didn't I?' Satisfied that she'd come down from her high, he lowered himself back down into the water and began to work her over again. He lightly nibbled upon her inner thighs, blew more bubbles gently across her sex and gave her only the lightest of teasing, tormenting touches with his tongue. His fingers pulled no punches, however. They worked inside her with a consistent rhythm and she was now copiously dribbling with her body's own lubrication, more than ready to feel his cock pounding away inside her. It would be, too.

At this moment in time he wanted this as much as she did. One might even argue more, but there was a reason behind his madness. Why was he intent on giving her so much pleasure when she had lavished him with nothing but pain in the last few years? The reasoning was simplicity in itself. Give her a taste of heaven, make her yearn for his every touch and then deny the very thing she had become addicted to, or at the very least, put her through the gates of hell in order to get it. Revenge, revenge, revenge; the word was always going to be uppermost in his mind with regard to his dealings with her. So she could have the ace of diamonds tonight, but come tomorrow, when she was tied up on his four-poster bed for the foreseeable future, unable to move more than a few centimetres in any direction; and suffering under his constant touch that aroused but never quite delivered, she'd be getting the joker. Oh, he would have fun with her all right.

Taking another sip of her saccharine sweetness he suckled gently, meanwhile letting his fingers pound into her core. Her taste was all over his mouth and it had a drugging effect on him. It made him want to suck her inside him whole, like a half-starved teenager.

He had to keep one arm underneath her body constantly now, because without it she would most certainly have drowned. She had little strength left and with his mouth attacking her sex like it was a Christmas dinner laden with all the trimmings, she could barely think straight let alone coordinate her limbs in an orderly fashion. His fingers stroked the inner walls of her slick channel, before his tongue thrust inside her, burrowing its way in as deep as it could go in order to sample the delights of her body. He put one finger on her clit and delicately rubbed as he drank from her sex. He heard the coiled scream in her throat getting ready to pounce, and then felt her body stiffening and her heartrate accelerated rapidly. He then pulled away brusquely and smiled down at her.

'How's that feel, precious?'

She did scream then, a tearing sound of frustration and woe. 'Don't stop,' she pleaded. 'Oh God, please don't stop.'

'You don't get to call the shots here. I'm in charge. You just need to follow my lead.' He winked at her and slowly licked his lips.

Violetta splashed at him frantically, her hands sending volleys of water cascading all over his body, but it hardly mattered as he was already soaked through.

'If that's the best you've got, sweetheart, you're going to have an extremely long night ahead of you.' Using both hands to scoop up a sizeable portion of water, he threw it at her over-sensitised sex.

Her mouth formed a pained 'O' shape and he watched the muscles of her pussy clench over and over again as she gasped out loud. Still no orgasm, but it was a close run thing. 'What do you want?' Her voice was thick with misery. Being denied intense pleasure did not suit her it seemed.

'I want you to beg me sweetly to continue and then I want your lips on my cock, showing their eagerness to return the favour. Think you can do that?'

'You want me to what?!' The woman looked as if ten thousand aliens had landed on the planet earth and just demanded that she take them to her leader. If they had, the little critters would have been in luck because he was right next to her.

He rolled his eyes. You'd almost have thought the woman was a twenty-four year old virgin... Well, it was time to set her straight. 'I want to get you on dry land. Actually, wet sand will do, and then I want you to drop to your knees, unfasten my fly, open your mouth and swallow me whole.' She looked at him blankly. It would have been funny, except at this moment in time it really wasn't. 'Goddamnit, just say "ahhh" and I can probably help you out with the rest. You agree to that and I'll let you have a taste of the good stuff. We set?' He raised his compulsive blue eyes to hers and allowed them to work their magic. The woman - why were women so damned awkward? - spewed out a gaggle of mismatched words, one of which could have been yes, and he was prepared to err on the side of recklessness. His patience was wearing thin, and it was strangely unlike him. He felt a roaring need to do the 'me Tarzan, you Jane' thing. It was slightly worrying. Her appeal would dwindle in the morning, he was sure of it. Right now he was looking forward to playing out their vision to the supreme satisfaction of both parties. He'd be generous and let her go first, though.

His tongue returned to her luscious nest of curls and foraged greedily for the sweet nectar within. This time he added a little more pressure, a tiny bit more friction and to make sure she felt it, a bit of G-spot stimulation. Inserting two fingers deep inside her he bent them into a 'C' shape and began beckoning her towards him with firm strokes. She sobbed. She begged. She thrashed. She writhed. She pleaded. She moaned, and then she begged some more.

'Come for me, baby,' he murmured against her wet flesh, 'come screaming.' He clamped his mouth tightly around her and suckled her little clit, flicking it with his tongue until he felt the earth move. It was the ocean, to be more exact, and it was caused by Violetta's flailing hands and thrashing limbs as she tossed around like a woman possessed. It seemed he'd found a woman with a bit of spirit - how utterly enchanting. He let her crash around happily, knowing that with his arm underneath her she wouldn't come to much harm, but his lips he kept pressed to her crotch until the very end. From the first violent convulsions as she initially tumbled over the edge, until he felt the last and weakest paroxysm subside from her body, he revelled in her every tremor. Never had he seen anything more beautiful. His huntress was a sight to behold in her soaking wet dress, the outline of her body stunningly depicted in dark brown silk, and the red glow to her newly awakened face brought out something primal within him. He felt his cock strain against his trousers and bit back a moan of intense torment. He'd get his in a moment, one way or another.

Waiting until she managed to catch her breath back, and giving her not a moment more, he said, 'You know you can stand up now, right, Vi? We've been in shallow water for the past ten minutes or so.'

His purring kitten changed her spots in the twinkling of an eye. There was an almighty roar of malcontent, some more splashing as she found her feet and then some fierce eyeballing as she made directly for him, her hands shaped into rather unattractive claws. His hellcat looked magnificent. The dress was now a second skin, her eyes radiated a decadent, lush heat that had only just been awakened and her hair, plastered tightly around her face gave her a fantastically sleek, sylphlike look. His mouth watered.

Oh, the things he was going to do to her when he got her back to his place. Imprison her, tie her up, deny her, tease and torment her. He was going to do all that and more. He was going to drive her insane, just as she had done to him, and when he finally tipped her over the edge he'd let her kill herself, if he was feeling generous. His desire for revenge was never very far from his thoughts and he intended to get even. Screw that. He intended to destroy her. There was a lot of hard work to get from this point in time to that, so he guessed he'd better get on with things, but at least his morose mood appeared to have lifted. Finally his life had purpose, goals and... a beautiful woman with which to play.

Deciding that the best and quickest course of action to get him where he wanted to go was to lead her to the shoreline, he waded quickly out of the waist-deep water and limbered up his muscles. Bringing his knees up high for a few strides, he made sure he was ready to take off when she managed to get close enough. The frantic splashing from behind told him all he needed to know. So he began to run, but took his time and adopted an unhurried pace. His huntress would be feeling a little tired from this evening's strenuous pursuits, and he didn't want her to expend all her energy just yet. She'd be needing a great deal of it in short order and he wanted to be shown a good time.

When his feet hit the soupy, syrupy sludge of the shallows, his toes had no time to wallow in the sand. He had a huntress on his back and she was coming at him with considerably more speed than he'd bargained on. He upped his pace. It wouldn't hurt to tire her out a little bit, he supposed. After all, she was after his blood.

He tossed his head over his shoulder and estimated she was about five metres or so away from him. He figured he'd wind her up a touch and raised his voice so that it carried loud enough to be heard behind him. 'Out of curiosity, why are you chasing me?'

'Because I'm going to kill you,' she roared, her hands still in those interestingly-shaped claws she'd formed earlier. He observed that she had the most incredibly long, bright pink nails and thought they should be one of the first things he got rid of, when he had her safely stowed away. The woman could take an eye out with those things, and while he was a vamp and he did heal, certain injuries were more painful than others.

'With what? Your bare hands? Good luck with that.' He sent her a playful wink. Many had tried, all had failed. He couldn't help but grin as she frantically slapped at her thighs. Ah ha, this is my vision, chérie, and I've had enough of stakes and knives for the time being. Her face suddenly lost all its colour as she realised she was unarmed and unable to deal with the large threat he presented.

'Oh, God.' Though his huntress was breathing hard, the words were clearly audible and the horror that surrounded them was unmistakable. It seemed she was a lady who rarely went anywhere without her weapons of destruction. Oops.

Although they were running along at quite a pace, she managed to turn abruptly on her heel as the stupidity of what she was trying to do sank in. She then took off at a hasty trot in the opposite direction. This was a much better result all round, in his opinion. He much preferred the chase from the vantage point of 'chaser', not least because he got to admire her tremendous buttocks as they wobbled in glorious unison, from left to right. Her dress hid nothing. She'd almost be better taking the thing off because it was hampering her running and she needed all the advantages she could get.

He let her sprint for a few minutes. The exercise wouldn't do her any harm. It was good for the heart, wouldn't you know? 'We're on an island in the middle of nowhere, precious. You can run, but you can't hide.' He watched as she put a little more velocity into her long stride and exulted in her pounding pulse. Being an omnipotent predator was a whole lot of fun sometimes. He could pounce upon her whenever he chose, because whilst she might be out of breath, he didn't require the substance and the speed they were currently travelling at was a slow walk in the park in vampire terms.

'Would you prefer to add another ten minutes on your workout, sweetness, or should I just jump you now? You did agree to this, remember?' He projected his words loud and clear, letting her know he was not in the least bit tired and could keep up with her ad nauseum if necessary, although he was sure it wouldn't be. Judging by her laboured breaths, his huntress was getting tired and that was exactly how he wanted her. It would make her just a little bit more pliable beneath him, when he tumbled her to the ground in a few seconds' time.

'If you call agreeing to have sex with a vampire while you're at risk of drowning a fair bargain you're out of your mind,' she bit back, one word at a time, as she fought for breath.

'Who said anything about fair? That kind of thing doesn't trouble us nocturnal types, princess, and you should really keep to your word when dealing with the undead. They play nasty when crossed.'

Deciding he'd had quite enough of the chase he pounced, his feet taking to the air in a burst of preternatural speed, and grabbing his huntress by the shoulders he flipped her over so she faced him, before smacking her down in the powder-white sand below. Fine, silvery grains sprayed everywhere.

He used a little more force than absolutely necessary to bang her into the ground. It wouldn't do her any harm if she was a little breathless and winded. The less aggravation he had to deal with the better, in his opinion. He was on top, she was beneath him, and that was pretty much how things were going to be from this moment forward. Unfortunately, being the gentleman that he was, he didn't do the job properly. She was still very much living and breathing beneath him and the girl intended to let him know how much she disapproved of his manhandling.

She fought him tooth and nail, but mainly nail, because he was careful not to let her teeth get near anything important. Those damn nails of hers had a party, though. They gouged into his chest, raking impressively long lines down his naked torso and that stung a little. After a little bit of a struggle, which he couldn't deny was most enjoyable, he managed to get a lock around both her wrists. Squeezing them tightly he slammed her fragile hands into the earth above her and scraped them along the sand until they were stretched out tight over her head. Her chest heaved with the exertion of trying to wriggle out from underneath him, but you didn't escape a vampire once they set their sights upon you. She was locked down, panting for breath and giving him some of the best evils he'd been fortunate enough to witness in his long and illustrious career as a member of the undead.

'Keep squirming like that and I'll be taking you with a bit more enthusiasm than I'd originally planned. Don't feel the need to stop on my behalf though; the feeling is most agreeable and my nether regions are applauding you most wholeheartedly.' She stopped all movement instantly, as was to be expected, and he gave a silent sigh of relief. There was only so much territory he could control within a vision, and she was making things difficult for him. It was rather ungenerous of her, considering this was her fantasy.

'Get off me.' Violetta had to battle to get those words past her lips. His body weight on top of hers was crushing the air space in her lungs.

'Say please.' His big blue eyes gave her a piercing look and blinked slowly. He felt the rush of heat that shot straight between her legs, even if she hadn't computed it yet.

'Your weight is killing me,' she managed to grate, through teeth clenched tightly in pain.

He gave her a lazy smile and bent down to kiss the tip of her nose. 'Don't make me repeat myself, princess.' To drive his point home he twisted his head to rest against the curve of her throat and scraped his teeth against the soft flesh of her neck.

'You promised!' The screech was impressive, considering he had yet to remove his weight from her body.

'Then play nicely and I might keep my end of the bargain.' He nipped at her jugular for good measure, to show he meant business.

'You win,' she squeaked, and her head scrabbled about frantically, trying to dislodge him. He kept his teeth exactly where they were. 'Please,' she added with a soft little whimper and a hiccup. Immediately raising his heavy frame from her body and supporting his weight on his knees, he was careful to keep a good hold of her hands. He wanted no further scrapes this evening, if at all possible.

'You're going to learn to obey me, princess,' he purred in her ear. 'You're going to learn to be silent unless spoken to, you're going to be trained to follow every command that leaves my lips as soon as it's issued and you won't even think of defying me. The consequences of failing will be far too high.'

'You'll have to kill me first,' she snapped back at him.

'It is a distinct possibility,' he agreed, and then let her raise both wrists a little as he moved into a more comfortable position, before crushing them back down into the grit and covering her mouth with his. He was not gentle. His lips crushed her lips and his tongue immediately caught hers in a whirlwind of motion. He didn't want that pretty little head of hers to think; she just needed to feel him. Hormones would take care of the rest.

At the first touch of his lips her eyes fluttered closed and her throat raised, almost in an act of surrender. At least one part of her body knew what it wanted. Wedging a thigh between her legs and pressing it up to her groin he heard a loud groan of pleasure. Perfect. Releasing one of her wrists quickly, but not softening the pressure of his mouth, he ripped the insubstantial elastic of her panties apart and flung them into the heavens beyond. She wouldn't be needing them for what he had in mind. Returning his hand to her wrist, amused that she had not even noticed its disappearance, he lowered his body once again over hers but did not transfer all of his weight. He was going to rub and grind against her for a few minutes and heat up all of that deliciously wet flesh.

Hard planes of muscles sinuously ground up along the twin mounds of her breasts and he let his thickened cock press against her silky smooth mound. The pleasure that coursed through him was indescribable. It would make life difficult for him later, but he was used to dealing with problems. They had become his middle name in the past few years.

Hearing a heated cry escape from her at his mouth's bruising treatment, and watching her back arch into the air he slowed the sucking motion of his lips. Giving her a chance to breathe and re-enter the kiss, he felt her gradually responding to him. His huntress settled down pretty quickly after that, the tiger becoming a veritable pussycat in less time than it would take the former to make breakfast out of the latter.

Speaking of breakfast, he realised his need for blood was growing. He couldn't remember the last time he'd fed, but being hungry kept him sharp and when you had a meeting with an infamous killer, you needed every edge you could get. She was going to keep him on his toes for a few days yet, he had little doubt, but not when her body had a fever that was raging hotter than hades. If he knew women, and *he knew women*, she'd be insensible for a while yet. Keeping the soft motions of his lips and tongue fluid he increased the weight of his body against hers, ever so slightly, to keep her in place as he got busy with other things. Releasing one of her wrists, he used his free hand to caress her breast through the sheer wet covering of her dress. He wanted to rip the thing off her with his bare hands and celebrate her form with his lips, tongue and fingertips, but he knew that would be too much for her to stand just yet, and he wasn't entirely sure he was up to the task without exploding, either. He smiled ruefully. This woman had taken him back hundreds of years in a single evening. How was that even possible? He'd had more notches than any normal bedpost could withstand. His control was legendary. He had women flocking to his door, and yet tonight he wanted to have a goddamn party in his pants. How irritating.

He straightened his jaw and applied himself diligently to the job before him. His fingertips tugged at her nipples, they gently smoothed the outline of her breasts and if the woman had a soul, which he very much doubted, he sucked the thing into him with each and every breath he took. Releasing her other wrist he let his hand tangle in her hair and realised he wanted her closer to him - much closer. Cradling the back of her neck in his hand and tugging at her locks he deepened his kiss once again, before pulling away to let his tongue stroke softly at her lower lips. She mewled pitifully as if in pain, and then grabbed both his shoulders in order to make him continue. He obliged, but gave her a nip on the lip to let her know that he was the one who dictated the moves, not her. It was a mistake. She opened her big violet eyes in shock, but her pupils were so dark and lust-filled he found himself instantly lost. Looking into those twin lilac portals he found himself wishing she was an immortal. Dangerous fucking territory. Snap out of it, he thought in disgust. Distance yourself.

But that was going to be a little hard with one hand pushing the wet silk of her skirt up her thighs, while the other reached down for his zipper. He wanted to feel flesh on flesh. This time there was no need to mess about and find out if she was wet. Judging by the thrashing motion of her head and arms, sending sand flying everywhere, she was more than ready and desperate for the slightest attention. The girl desired to be used and it was safe to say he was about to give her exactly what she wanted, if she knew what she wanted, which she didn't.

He pulled his face away from hers and they both took a minute to regain their composure. She needed to catch her breath, and he needed to get a grip on himself, which was, quite frankly, annoying.

'Get up,' he ordered roughly, and it was clear it was in no way a question, for he had her hands tightly in his and was using them to pull her body upright. When she was on two feet he let her go but noticed she was more than a little unsteady on her feet. 'Lose the dress.' Another command. He almost felt like his old self again. Now to wait and see whether she would obey. Actually, that was a lie. He knew she wouldn't take off the damn dress and wasn't that going to be half the fun? 'Lose the dress now or I'll rip it from your body and make you walk back to the hotel naked. Sex and sand do not mix.' He watched her hesitate as he knew she would, and he stalked forward to do exactly as he'd threatened. The look on his face was monstrous; he'd had plenty of years to perfect it. She looked around desperately, as if seeking a place of refuge, but the woman wasn't stupid. She couldn't outrun him, she couldn't fight him, and if she were brutally honest, she'd realise she didn't want to. Her body belonged to his. He'd concentrate on warping her mind over to the dark side later, but for now, her body would do.

As both of his hands reached forward to grab the neckline of her dress and found the limp, almost translucent fabric, he saw her body shake. He would need to get her close to him again. Lots of skin contact would make her docile and mindless, and stem the shock that was threatening to overwhelm her. That meant he had little time to spare. His hands flew in opposite directions and a loud tearing sound lit up the night air.

'Stop!' She'd managed to yell the sound at the top of her lungs and it surprised him enough, that he needed to take a step back from her. The expression on her face was one of defeat. With her eyes darting to and fro, sizing up all of her non-existent options, she had nowhere to go. Placing her hands in the air, as if they might ward him away, he watched intently as a fit of tremors overtook her fingers, before she slowly lowered them in order to roll up the edge of her dress. There was then a lengthy pause, which he mightily disapproved of, before she began to pull the dripping fabric upward. He wanted to stand dispassionately and admire her shapely figure, in the normal way he would appreciate one of his bedfellows. When the dress hitched over her mid-thighs he thought he was doing quite well, too. His heartrate had only increased by a couple of beats per minute, so that wasn't bad all in all. Alas, the woman had to work hard to get out of the soaking material and when she began to shimmy back and forth, he felt his central incisors try to take a chunk out of his bottom lip. Her backside wiggled, her breasts bounced and as he dug his toes into the wet sand he had to bite down, causing a good degree of physical pain, in order to make sure he stayed where he was and didn't go gung-ho and flatten her straight back into the ground. When the hem of her dress wavered above her sex he swallowed thickly. She had a shockingly beautiful physique and the need to bury himself inside her grew to rather painful proportions. If the bloody woman didn't get a move on he was going back to the original idea of ripping the dress from end to end.

The thing slithered up her stomach, displaying a concave stomach and creamy white flesh utterly devoid of a single blemish. She was perfect in every way and she was his. *His, his, his.* Since when had he been so territorial? Up and up the silk rose, twisting and pulling against her damp flesh, and then she was completely naked, utterly vulnerable and boy, oh boy, was he going to take advantage of her. Without another word he grabbed her hand and dragged her back to the water's edge.

'No, not back in...' but her querulous little complaint was stopped in mid-flow as his lips claimed hers. His arms hoisted her into the air effortlessly and he wrapped her legs around his waist. She could conserve her energy for now, because in a few moments she'd be requiring all the reserves she had. Together they waded back into the tepid ocean, with her arms tight around his neck and their faces locked together. His cock pressed against her naked sex and grew with every step he took. The tell-tale quivers of her body told him all he needed to know in return. His huntress was ripe for the taking and ready to be introduced to the wonders of coitus. He was more than happy to oblige her. Removing his hands from her waist he shucked out of his trousers and pants. He wasn't worried that she might fall in, the grip she had around his neck was merciless and her nails were digging into his flesh in heated anticipation of what was to come. The negligible pain spurred him on and he found himself scoring the tips of his fingers up her back and arching her down towards the water as he positioned the entrance of her sex directly over the head of his cock. He didn't enter her, but just let himself pulse against her; the tip seeking a warm home in which to bury itself would do the job of introductions very nicely. She moaned. A throaty moan directed straight into his ear, and as her teeth grazed his lips he couldn't help himself. He surged forward inside her.

She was so goddamn tight and wet he thought he'd lose it. Her vaginal muscles clamped around him with an iron-grip and sucked him inside, but nowhere near far enough. Of course. His precious princess was a virgin. That was easily remedied, though. Using his hands as leverage around her waist once more, he began to gently pump inside her. He used slow, tiny motions that had her rocking back and forth against him as his hands migrated to her backside, in order to get a better grip for what he was about to do. She'd given up trying to kiss him, her thoughts were all over the place as desire began to flood her body, and if only she knew what she needed his little kitten would have taken it by now. Her inexperience had her bouncing back and forward on the knife edge to climax, caught inside a delirious mix of pleasure and pain. As she buried her face in his neck and began to lap at his flesh, he knew it was time.

Placing his finger on her clit and rubbing furiously he surged, breaking through the barrier of her hymen in a single thrust, but not giving her a single second to process the pain. Flinging her body down on his, over and over again, grinding himself against her little nub of sensory nerve-endings, he knew she would be airborne in another three or four of her franticly pulsing heartbeats. The pressure against his neck increased. The damn chit was going to give him a hickey if she kept that up, but hell if he cared. He bounced her up and down with skill, getting a little faster and a touch harder with every lunge of their bodies. Another thrust and they both tumbled into the black heart of oblivion, and he was only sorry that the stay would be such a short one.

Feeling himself spurt into her he felt oddly groggy, and the pleasure which was usually short-lived seemed to go on and on. He felt her convulse around him, her muscles squeezing down upon his cock, milking him dry as her body gave in to one of the most intense sensations she had ever felt in her short existence. Feeling increasingly dizzy as he emptied himself, he was only just aware of a continuing pain in his neck. What on earth was the crazy woman up to now? Biting him? Using a hand to try and bat her away from him he just managed to make out a finger and thumb as his hand uselessly flopped back. Too late, he realised she had dug her fingers into his neck and managed to get his carotid artery in a pincer grip. If he wasn't much mistaken his blood pressure was just about to hit the floor. As his vision went double he managed to summon just enough energy to wrench her away from him, splashing back into the sea to put some distance between them. She came at him again, but a few precious moments was all he needed to put his world back in colour. Snarling, he reached forward and grabbed her by the hair. Twisting her neck fiercely in his hands and bringing her flesh up to his mouth, he plunged his fangs deep.

Gondolas

Before the force and intense pleasure of his bite had the chance to hit home, he released her from his vision abruptly. She was sobbing pathetically, from the knowledge that he had stripped her of her virginity and the ability to perform her day job in one foul swoop. It would take her a few seconds to realise that her travels had been nothing more than a pleasant delusion, but for now his work was done. Her body shook uncontrollably in the awkward position she held, still bent over double from the waist. It would have been an almost comical sight, had he not found her behaviour maddening beyond disbelief. In the throes of passion his little princess had been plotting his demise. That was a first. Never before had his performance been so lacklustre that someone had managed to nearly kill him during the event. He was mightily peeved by the whole situation. His prowess in the bedroom department was legendary. What on earth was wrong with her? Grinding his teeth in annoyance, he realised there were other things he should be concentrating on.

Zeroing in on the little vial she still carried, gripped tightly between trembling fingers, he noted with some small semblance of satisfaction that they had little control or coordination to keep it safe for much longer. Her body pulsed and contracted in the throes of one of the most powerful climaxes known to the female kind, and he should know. He'd perfected his technique over several centuries. Unfortunately she could still function perfectly throughout the procedure. Doling out death was far more important than appreciating pleasure, apparently. Martinet was still seething. The woman should not have been able to operate in any conceivable way as he brought her to climax. It meant he was not doing the job properly, and he always delivered the goods. He knew her body had climaxed hard against him, was sure of it, yet still couldn't believe that she'd been concentrating on killing him the whole time she'd been riding him. It left him cold. What did he expect though? She was a trained murderess. This was second nature to her. It mattered not that she'd been a virgin. There was only one thought in her head and that was to kill. Getting a grip on himself, he returned his attention to the tiny glass bottle. He needed to keep his wits about him around Violetta, and he would do well to remember the fact.

His eyes descended to the tube, which was shaking madly and he knew that at least one aspect of his plans was going to come to fruition. Another couple of convulsions and the vial would no longer be a problem. Admiring the shape of her delectable buttocks as they swayed to and fro, and the beautiful twist of her mouth as she cried out, he watched intently as the vial began to slip slowly through her fingers - fingers already slick with sweat. The little ampoule didn't stand a chance. Even if it had she'd have less strength than a butterfly flowing through her stretched, tortured limbs. It would take a few moments for her circulation to return. She suffered another seizure of pleasure on a grand mal scale and her limbs flew everywhere, in helpless abandon. The vial then sailed out of her fingers and headed south. Victory was his.

He was certainly racking some points up this evening, but he was smart enough to realise that he would need to be constantly on his toes around the huntress. Suspecting that determination would be her middle name, he reckoned he could wipe the smile off her face within a week or two, if she was given the right incentive. He hoped she'd rise to the challenge of sexually entertaining a vampire master before long, or he was sure to become rather jaded with her presence. Time would tell. On the plus side, humans were pathetically easy to kill and he'd probably be able to dispose of her with relative ease.

A splintering sound was heard, exploding inside his finely-tuned eardrums like the opening bar of a marching band, his head whipping round in horror. The vial should have landed safely on the grass, where it would remain whole and intact. His jaw dropped as he realised his error. He had thrown her silver dagger carelessly between her feet, little more than a few seconds ago, and unbelievably the tiny bottle had found the only thing it could smash itself upon in the garden. Could she have directed it there, in the state she was in? The thought was an impossible one. She was in no fit state to do anything. Be that as it may, tiny droplets exploded all around him in horrific clarity, and he could not escape a single one of them. They froze in his vision for a split second in time, letting him know they were going to fly everywhere, and he knew they were going to do some damage.

As the first fleck of fluid landed on his leg he waited in disagreeable anticipation for the pain to hit. He was not to be disappointed. Her friends were at least wise enough to have doctored the water with something unpleasant. Garlic oil. The stuff was the equivalent of dropping hydrochloric acid on a human, and it burned and sizzled just as nastily. It wouldn't kill him, but he'd learnt long ago that pain and death did not necessarily follow hand in hand. The worst part about this ordeal was that he had to keep his mind sharp to control the girl, whilst making sure she didn't have an inkling of what the water did to his kind. If he made out the water was harmless she was unlikely to try the same trick again. It was a good theory, but putting on a show of nonchalance for her benefit was going to take all of his formidable resolve and more. The drops sank into the material of his trousers and burned into his flesh. He could have ripped them off to lessen the damage, but it would have made little difference. The worst had been done and all he could do now was try to ensure it never happened again. Giving himself a moment before trusting himself to speak, he allowed her the privilege of standing upright once more.

Slowly raising his eyes to hers, he said, 'So I guess that means you can cross stakes, silver, and holy water off your list of rapidly diminishing death-delivering items.' The words came out reasonably steadily, and for that he was thankful. The garlic oil was beginning to do its thing upon his legs and in quite spectacular fashion, but he still managed his trademark smile at the end of the sentence. Only a fellow vampire would have been able to spot the tiny strains of discomfort that had begun to tighten his facial expression.

'You bit me,' she accused, aghast, her mouth pulled back in a grimace of horror.

'Oh, do keep up,' he said with a tired sigh. 'I pretended to bite you. That little morsel of fun happened only inside your head. The real thing is far better, and if you're a good girl I might even give you a demonstration.' There was no accompanying smile after the sentence, and didn't that say it all?

'No, you bit me, earlier.' Her voice was rising and sounded slightly hysterical. 'My knife,' she pointed to the blade between her feet, 'is covered in blood. My shoulder stings. You bit me.'

'Pumpkin,' he sighed, 'you'd know if I bit you. There'd be a post-orgasmic, flashing blue lights, shocked-at-the-brilliance of the world type of aura about you. All you've had is a knife plunged into your shoulder. If you're hankering after a set of puncture wounds though, I'm sure I can oblige.' He used his index finger to beckon her forward and displayed a set of prominent fangs for her benefit. 'It's jolly good...'

'Fine.' She managed to get her trembling hands under control and used them to smooth her auburn waves carefully around her face. Rearranging the long folds of her dress, which had become decidedly rumpled as she'd worn them dangling around her face for the duration of the spanking, she then took great care to pick up the knife by its unsullied handle and looked at it with displeasure.

'You be a good girl and give it to your friends. You know exactly what will happen if you don't, princess.' He waved her back into the ballroom beyond, where a lively orchestral tune had just struck up. Her face turned to the lights streaming through the open doors and he knew she wanted to make a break for the safety of the walls within. She had much to learn. Nowhere would be safe for her any more. In fact, safety would not be a usable word in her vocabulary from this night forth. 'After you've finished with your death buddies, come back here and we'll go party at mine. I'll show you what you've been missing all these years.' He unearthed his fangs again for good measure, and curled his tongue around a sharp point.

He knew she had to bite down the urge to scream at him. It would have been immensely entertaining had he not been coping with third degree burns.

'You wouldn't want to give me any hints or tips on how to remove that arrogant head of yours from your body, would you?' Her voice held a simpering, sweet quality, and her little girl antics made him want to throw her down on the ground and cover her entire body with grass stains.

'What can I say?' He shrugged. 'You'll probably need to take a step over into the other side of life to find out though. You'll never kill me as a human.'

'You're the most vile and loathsome creature I've ever met, Martinet. Using my fantasy was a low blow. Sexy stranger you may be, but you were hardly a knight in shining armour. Next time you grope around for fantasies inside my head make sure you do the job properly,' she barked.

'You came, didn't you? What more do you want? Rose petals and a fanfare? Tell you what, next time I'll get out the horse and carriage and we can go for a proper ride...' Martinet didn't bother continuing. He was presented with her back as she stomped off, and damned if she didn't have a mighty fine ass to ogle.

'Your performance was appalling, by the way.' She did not raise her voice to utter the condemning statement, but she was well aware that she didn't need to. What was it with women who always needed to get the last word in?

He cupped his hands around his mouth and yelled, 'Good thing I'll be getting

64

plenty of practise in later then, isn't it?' He had to raise his voice quite significantly to make sure he could be heard by her inferior ears. No reply was forthcoming, but he knew she'd heard him by the stiffening of her neck and the tightening of her fingers. Alas, she didn't quite manage to hide the infuriated shriek that burst forth from her lips and refused to be stoppered by both of her similarly maddened hands. Increasing her already rather fast pace she continued to stalk off towards the welcoming light of the ballroom, giving him not so much as a second glance.

The Duchess stepped silently out of the shadows and almost startled him, which was shocking in itself. The girl had made him forget about everything else around him, including, most importantly, that the whole scene had been witnessed.

'Are you OK, darling?'

'Never better, Maggie. I have a thing about virgins, wouldn't you know? Well done for spotting that little titbit. You're a sharp creature, aren't you?'

'I can smell the garlic from here, Michel.' She sniffed the air as if to emphasize her point. 'The girl's gone and there is no one left to impress. You don't have to pretend for my benefit.'

'I'm impervious to pain, Maggie.' Martinet gave her a bored look. She would always suspect, but she'd never know it was a lie for certain, and that suited him just fine. Vampire politics were difficult things. Her answering snort told him all he needed to know on that score, unfortunately.

'You are just as magnificent as they say you are,' she said cheekily, giving him a sly wink as she walked calmly away, slinking back into the shadows with a speed and agility that belied her venerable age. She didn't finish the conversation on words of praise, however. 'You do know she's going to run, don't you?'

'Oh, I'm counting on it,' he replied.

There was a titter of laughter and then the Duchess disappeared from his life as quickly as she had entered it. And she did manage to get the last word in. 'Run for your life, precious,' she whispered softly on the wind. It was clear that her last sentence was not for him. Trust the Duchess to be on the side of the underdog.

Women, muttered Martinet, rolling his eyes in annoyance. He had to hand it to her, though. Never before had the sentence seemed more apt...

Details

Violetta wanted to pull things apart. She wanted to curse and rail, stomp and tear, and she wouldn't have been averse to letting a nuclear bomb explode at this moment in time, even if it took out most of the Provincia di Venezia with it. She had never felt quite so impotent in all her life. He held all the cards, every single one, and there didn't appear to be a single thing she could do about it.

Curling the blood-soaked knife into the back of her hand and concealing it within the folds of her dress, she began to forge a path through the patrons of the ballroom. The bright sparkle of the crystal chandeliers was the first thing to catch her eye and it dragged her head upward, where she admired the elegant frescos that adorned the ceilings. Cherubs danced in sunny blue skies and the intricate, gilded plasterwork that contained them almost took the beauty of the images away. The impressive room was made up of an array of archways featuring tall, rectangular, mullioned windows, and these were decorated with elaborate cream drapes and pelmets. The lighting was soft and provided a warm glow to the dancers below, but there was no mistaking the energy of the room, even if you discounted the lively tune the string quartet had just struck up.

Due to the lateness of the hour and the free bar situated to the rear of the Castello, the dancers were looking a little less formal than they had at the beginning of the evening. Bow-ties were hanging around necks, top buttons had been unfastened and shirt lapels pulled wide apart to ease the heat that now pervaded the length and breadth of the hall, and that was just the men. Some of the women had lost their masks, and others were wearing their feathered and sparkled creations at a rather unseemly angle. Skirts had been hitched up, necklines had been dipped and a few had taken to dancing barefoot. Violetta would not have recognised the glazed looks on the women's faces before her dealings with Monsieur Martinet, but now she knew all too well what those dark, almost feverish glances meant. Here was a dance hall in heat and they all had one thing on their minds.

Images of Martinet came flooding back to her, and she had no idea whether it was her weak-willed mind that had placed them there or whether he was doctoring things from his end. Her broken arm did not hurt, so she knew he was still inside her, monitoring her every move, but she had no idea how much control he had over her thoughts. Oh God, that was a lie. Judging by the way he'd manipulated her fantasy and got inside her head, he had total control of them. The thought was both mind-blowing and horrific. How could one single being wield so much power?

When one gentleman partygoer made to stand in front of her and proffered his hand for a dance, she took one long look at him and the arm was swiftly withdrawn. She'd had more than her fair share of the male species for this evening and she wasn't going to go near them for the foreseeable future. Pushing past him with renewed purpose, she set about her task. Her colleagues were waiting for her with great big smiles of undisguisable glee lighting up their faces, ready for good news. If only they knew. Plastering a weak smile to her face, which she felt subtly widened by her vampire antagonist, she tried to look suitably euphoric. A vampire kill would inspire those powerful and compelling emotions inside her and she could do nothing less than convince them of her magnificent success. If she failed, she had no doubt that Martinet would do exactly as he had threatened and massacre the lot of them. Whilst Violetta knew they did not fear death, she could not have that on her conscience. Their group was one of the few bands of vampire hunters left in the world, and if it disappeared overnight in its entirety the world would rock on its heels. It would leave vampires, such as Martinet, with a safe breeding ground to increase their numbers exponentially, and she could not allow that to happen. The human race had to be protected at all costs. A world of bloodsucking monsters was unthinkable.

Withdrawing the silver dagger from the floaty folds of her skirt she passed it to Connaught, her smile of satisfaction for a job well done entirely Martinet's creation. Her eyes gleamed with accomplishment and pleasure.

'Was he hard to kill?' Connaught wasn't looking at her face; he was examining the blood on her knife in greater detail. It was almost as if he didn't believe she had killed him.

'He was very hard, yes.' The words that tripped out of Violetta's mouth were not her own and she was not impressed at the vision of Martinet's body that swam before her eyes. The hard planes of his chest, the sculpted muscles that burst from his abdomen in beautiful lines, and if one cared to look lower, there were other, *hard* things. Violetta was unamused but the sentiment did not show upon her face.

Connaught had slipped a finger into the lines of swiftly congealing blood and he brought it to his nose to inhale its scent. He frowned. 'Doesn't smell as coppery as it should and it's not quite as thick as I'd expect.' Handing the knife back, he gave her a puzzled look.

'He was a master, Con. His blood will be purer and thinner.'

Con's expression turned into one of disbelief. His tongue lolled about uselessly in his mouth for a moment before he recovered the gift of speech. 'He was a what?'

Violetta knew there was no need for her to repeat the statement. Con just needed a few moments to process the thought on his own. Darla, who did not suffer from the same reticence as her peer, burst in with, 'Did he have the gift?'

Huddled in their own little corner you would have thought they were a group of old ladies discussing village gossip. Darla was interested in power, Georgette wanted to know if she'd just killed a handsome hunk, and Rafael had tactics on his mind. A barrage of questions invaded her head and she wanted to shut them all out. She wanted to physically slap her hands over her ears and scream at them to shut up. All Violetta wanted to do was run far, far away from everybody. Oh, if only that were possible. Martinet kept her smiling sweetly and chatting away animatedly, answering all their questions with an enthusiasm that said 'I've killed tonight and oh boy, I've enjoyed myself'.

'How did you kill him?' Con asked the most pertinent question, as always. His intelligent grey eyes tilted up towards the light and his whole face creased in concentration as he tried to figure out how a little slip of a girl like Violetta could kill a hardened, master vampire and come gliding back into the ballroom without a mark upon her.

She had no idea how to answer that question, considering she was still working on the schematics of how to do the deed herself. Martinet, adorable creature that he was, provided an answer for her.

'Quickly.'

'You must be joking,' she thought grimly in reply. 'I'll make sure it's drawn out and hideously painful.'

He replied in kind, 'I'll remember that when the time comes to kill you, chérie. Drawn out and hideously painful suits me just fine. Whether it'll look just as good on you is another matter entirely.'

Violetta waited for him to laugh, but he was obviously short on humour as the evening wore on, due to the ominous silence his end.

'Was he attractive?' Georgette, who was wearing the most expansive pink ball-gown that had graced the halls of the Castello, in at least the last one hundred years or so, had only one thing on her mind. Whilst the woman couldn't have been a day under sixty-five, and if rumours were to be believed she was considerably older, she was quite the feisty one. Primping one of her pristine grey ringlets in her hand, she winked slyly. 'You know I need details. When you get to my age life suddenly gets very dull. When men get to my age they become even duller, so I like to live vicariously through young little starlets such as yourself. So don't keep an old lady waiting. Was he dishy?'

Violetta could have groaned out loud at Georgette's persistence, Connaught looked embarrassed and Darla gave a big groan of annoyance. Rafael, casually propped against the wall with one leg, looked at her with an insouciant, heavy-lidded half-smile. 'Come on, Violet, was he everything you'd ever dreamt of? Set Georgette's mind at rest and we can get on to discussing the more interesting stuff.'

Glaring at the beautiful Rafael, while resisting the urge to kick him, she had a moment's pause to realise that the man was probably the antithesis of Michel Martinet. Short blond curls, deep chestnut eyes and a vivacious love of life that nearly always kept him in good spirits, gave him the face and temperament of an angel. His sense of humour, however, could be likened to Martinet's. It was sarcastic, cutting and often horribly dry.

'Do tell us, Violet. Was he terribly hideous or delightfully gorgeous?' It was clear that Georgette was not about to let the question go until she received a satisfactory answer. Raising an ornate black-lacquered Japanese fan to her face, she began to swish it about in frantic flurries, sending her ringlets flying. The pretty petals of pale pink cherry blossom that had been painted onto each rib of the fan appeared to blur into one as Georgette swung it to and fro, wafting undercurrents of her perfume to the room's occupants, which was a little overpowering at close range.

Violetta took a step back and decided she did not want to answer that question at all. Especially seeing as how dear old monster vamp was sucking up and drinking in every word they were saying. Keeping very quiet, she wondered if he'd answer it for her. She attuned her ears to the loud chatter of the ballroom beyond and watched the swing and sway of the brightly coloured dancers as they whirled around the floor. No such luck. Her lips did not move an inch. Georgette, however, kept the fan flickering at high speed, and if the question wasn't answered shortly her old-fashioned attempt at air-conditioning might just manage to take her wig off.

There were really only two options to her dilemma. She could either ignore the question, knowing she would never hear the end of it, or she could answer it and have her face explode in heat, giving the assembled hunters a good laugh at her expense. On second thoughts, maybe there were three options. She could always lie.

'I'm not going to allow you to lie, precious,' came the ominous, I'm-always-going-to-be-in-your-head voice. 'You should know that naughty girls who tell fibs get spanked. I have no problem baring that delightful backside of yours for another round of hand tennis and you might also be interested to know that I've won awards in the subject. I'm a veritable John McEnroe.'

Violetta might have noticed the slightly strained quality of Martinet's voice had her brain not been about to explode. The man was conceited, obnoxious and insufferable. He was going to drive her insane. Breathing in deeply she tried to think her way around the problem. In through the nose and out through the mouth. Lie, cheat or ignore. In through the nose and out through the mouth. Lying seemed like the obvious choice. Smiling sweetly at Georgette, she opened her mouth and prepared to tell the assembled small crowd of hunters how truly dreadful and unsightly her master vamp was. The threat of a spanking did not quell her spirit in the slightest. If she had to dance with the devil, it certainly didn't mean she had to sing his tune.

The trouble was, when she opened her mouth to deliver her best acting performance to date, not a word of sound escaped her lips. Looking rather like a goldfish on the hunt for food, Violetta realised if she continued trying to form words with no sound issuing from her lips, her comrades were going to think she had gone mad. The urge to stomp her foot like a three year old toddler having a tantrum was also not going to do much for her reputation. It appeared he had left her no option. It was to be the truth or nothing. Never before had she wanted to murder a being quite so much as she did right now, but that was probably not going to be fresh news to him, nor would it give him a reason to quake in his boots. The vamp knew exactly what she was about and found controlling her every move so very easy, he would probably be able to do it backwards in his sleep. Bastard. She refused to give in that easily. There had to be some way out of this mess... and then it came to her. Smiling, mostly by herself, for the first time since she'd met Monsieur Martinet, she straightened her shoulders and elongated her beautifully swan-like neck to its highest proportions. Let the vamp suck on this, she thought.

'I suppose he was reasonably attractive in a vampire sort of way.' The words came out beautifully. All elegant, aloof and slightly snooty, and then her face immediately went bright red as she had known it would, spoiling the whole damn effect. Glowing like a flaming beacon in the night, her half-truth was immediately spotted. Rafael snorted and Georgette clapped her hands and beamed from ear to ear.

'I knew it! He was hopelessly gorgeous!' There was a loud squeal of delight before several metres of bright pink crinoline skirt swirled around in a complete circle, tornado style, and once the whirlwind had started it was clear it was going to need some help in order to halt its progress. In the end Rafael came to the rescue, grabbing Georgette around the waist and squeezing the bulging material tightly around her to dispel some of the storm wind that had gathered. There was a round of applause at his attempt of gallantry and he even managed to straighten her wig, which had managed to rest at a jaunty angle over one eye. 'Georgie, for heaven's sake sit down. Violet's just killed a master vamp, she hasn't managed to accomplish world domination. Yet,' he added for good measure with a wink.

The elderly dame was deposited in a plush red velvet Queen Anne style chair, and she landed with quite a thump. Not in the least bit daunted by her close call with a hard and unforgiving parquet floor, she once again turned to her friend and barked, 'Details!'

Violetta glowered, lowered her eyes and clamped her jaw together. She was not about to big up the vamp who already had the kind of inflated ego that would rival a hot air balloon, to say the least. Georgette would just have to remain clueless for once. So she hummed to herself quietly and examined her bright pink nail polish, which had a few scratches after tonight's rather energetic escapades.

'Violet, for goodness sake look at me and then answer me, dammit. You know I don't get out much and you need details when you get to my age.' Georgette clucked her tongue and gave her that hurt, disappointed expression she reserved for particularly fractious children.

Violetta continued to look at the floor, which had a really interesting wood grain - it was probably oak but could possibly have been maple, at a pinch. Her ruse was to try and pretend that she hadn't heard a word. Of course it didn't work, but it wasn't Georgette who pulled her up on her wayward behaviour. Her eyes stopped examining the wooden floor panels and pulled themselves rapidly upward, whilst her mouth took on a beatific smile. Her hands removed themselves from lounging behind the back of her dress, to resting gently clasped together in front of her. Her posture was also undergoing immediate improvement and she was beginning to feel like someone had rammed a broomstick up her backside. Shoulders were subtly straightening themselves, butt cheeks and abdomen were being sucked in to waif-like proportions, and her neck was beginning to lean forward towards Georgette in an almost conspiratorial fashion. She did not have a good feeling about this. When her lips began to move things went from bad to worse.

'Georgie,' she simpered, batting her eyelashes, 'he had the most adorable hair. Silky strands of soft, touchable, ebony waves that curled lightly around his neck. Add to that high, aristocratic cheek bones and the most piercing blue eyes you have ever seen. I almost cried when I had to kill him.' Violetta had already been incensed at being used as his own personal puppet once again, but after that remark she wanted to punch rather large holes all over his body with a jack hammer. She wasn't sure he'd deflate after the ordeal but she'd sure feel a hell of a lot better. She heard him tsk inside her head, as if telling off a naughty child before she felt a hand run down her backside. Only just managing to stop her body jumping up in panic, she had an equally hard time trying to stop the curse that wanted to explode from her lips. It wasn't as hard a task as she feared. Horrifically, they were going to continue to spew their ridiculous drivel. 'Oh and muscles, Georgie, he was positively bursting with the things. He had a washboard abdomen that clothes would have paid to be cleaned upon. Nice bum, squishy in all the right places, but his best feature by far was his eyes.' Her hands began waving around at that point, to make it clear to her audience she was fully involved in the conversation and enjoying herself. Oh God, why didn't he just tear her vein out now? But the madness continued. 'They lit up the night sky, Georgette. Think of the deepest blue you can imagine, a clear summer's sky at twilight, perhaps, and then add a luminous, shining heat behind them. They were eyes that ate women for breakfast, lunch and dinner, two at a time. You could spend a whole day gazing into them and never grow bored. He was divine. The beast was deiform in every possible way that could matter and if I'm honest, I could hardly contemplate killing him.' If it wasn't enough to have to choke down the bile that would have threatened to spill at that statement, had it been allowed to, she could now feel beads of teardrops begin to pool in the corners of her eyes. Her indignity was to know no bounds, it seemed. Looking terribly distraught, she waved her hands in the air as if that might stop her from crying and gave a choked apology to her shell-shocked collection of friends. 'I'm sorry everyone. I think I need to turn in for the evening. It's been a long night and I'm exhausted. In the morning I'll be right as rain, but I think I need to rest up now.'

The entire group looked at her sympathetically, with the exception of Rafael. He used the foot he was balancing on to push himself away from the wall and he walked towards her, smiling lazily.

'You've never been this upset after killing a vamp before, Violet. You're not losing your touch, are you?' He picked up a tendril of her bright orange hair and caressed it gently in his fingertips. Violetta moaned softly and wished he would walk right back to where he had come from. She'd had more than enough stimulation from attractive men this evening and she didn't need any more. 'Was he more beautiful than me, Violet? Did he set your heart aflame?' The question was dark and mocking, but there were glowing embers in Rafael's eyes which spoke of something else entirely.

Wishing she was more experienced in the ways of men, at least enough to decipher them a little better, she once again felt her lips move, and the automatic reaction of clamping her hands over her face carried upward to her brain before it was immediately snuffed out by Martinet.

'Much, much more beautiful than you,' she heard herself say in horror, which was closely followed by, 'and he certainly set something on fire.' For some reason unbeknownst to her, she felt her legs once again under her own control and deciding not to tempt fate, she used them, quickly. Waving a hasty goodbye to the ladies and gentleman who had crowded around her, hoping for splendid tales of blood and gore, she pushed through the swathes in a blind panic. Her need to escape was great.

Dashing through the see of faces she noticed Georgette's eyes were still goggling with fascination, Connaught looked somewhat concerned at her hasty departure, and Rafael? Well, he looked faintly amused. The tips of his fingers lightly skimmed her forearm as she brushed past him and she spun around to watch his gaze narrow as his eyes feasted upon her. It was a look she instantly recognised, having only just recently discovered it, and damned if it didn't make her run even faster.

A Bid for Freedom

It was all she could do not to break into a fast run as soon as her feet hit the gravel drive of the Castello, but running would attract the kind of attention she did not need, so even though all instincts were screaming at her to make a break for it, she reigned herself in. She did not turn her head to admire the elegant stone portico reception with its high plasterwork arches and intricate artwork, she did not stop to retrieve her beautiful shot silk shawl that had been deposited with a coatroom attendant on arrival, and she did not respond to any of the eager male glances being directed her way. She'd had quite enough of men for the evening.

Concentrating on weaving her way between the tiny borders of the boxed hedge garden, she made her way past trumpeting angels spouting fountains of water and large topiary arrangements of neatly clipped, cone-shaped trees. The front of the Castello walls had a panel of hedging that had been arranged into crenelated lines, resembling that of a fortress. It would have been a beautiful sight to behold had she not had her mind on other things. Listening to the grit crunch below her feet she slipped and skidded, but she barely noticed. Her gaze was set on the soft glow of lamplight from the street just beyond the imposing cast-iron entrance gates, and she walked as fast as her legs would allow her. When she finally reached the solace of the cobbled street and the castle gates had disappeared from view, she broke into a sprint and let her feet fly.

The adrenaline running through her body was at overload status. Every sense was on high alert. She listened for the tiniest sounds, kept her eyes peeled to all that was going on around her and embraced the cool night air as it whipped her hair from her face. Violetta had a plan.

It was a relatively simple one. She needed to get herself inside hallowed walls, and those of St Mark's Basilica would work very nicely. He could not follow her inside there. No vampire alive would ever willingly step inside those holy walls.

In her rush to escape she found her bare feet tumbling over uneven cobblestones, but she refused to slow her pace. Time would be of the essence. Even though she was carefully guarding her thoughts, Martinet would soon realise that the image of herself chatting to her friends in the grand ballroom was a false one and there was only so much chatter and small talk that could be invented by one mind alone. If she concentrated she might gain ten minutes. It might sound like a long time, but to a vampire that could move at the speed of light and travel with the wind, it was no time at all. He'd be able to make up the distance in the blink of an eyelid.

As her next footfall landed her shoulder gave out a sharp jolt of pain. It made her gasp but did not slow her down. Distance, it appeared, would have its own pitfalls. It was quite possible that the vampire could only provide pain management and mind control if she were nearby, thus the more distance she managed to place between herself and the beast, the more her shoulder would pain her. She was soon going to find out, one way or another.

'Distance isn't much of an object for me, now that a drop of my venom is in your veins and you can finish with the delightful drivel you are currently pretending to voice to Georgette. Your friends left the building five minutes ago.'

The sound of his gravelly voice in her head had her gulping for breath and stumbling simultaneously. She immediately panicked. There would be no time. His hands would be all over her in an instant and she would be destined for nowhere but death. Her body teetered forward, balance skewed drastically to the right, before she managed to steady herself.

'Don't stop on my account, princess,' he purred darkly. 'I've got to pick up my coat. That should give you a fighting head start, ma chérie. No one rushes around in Italy, bar you apparently.' There was a small pause as he cleared his throat. 'Oh, one more thing. As you blatantly disregarded my instructions, the pain management stops. Consider it part of your punishment, although we'll work on some finer aspects of correctional behaviour later this evening. If you think that bottom of yours stings now, you wait until I've finished with it this time tomorrow. That purple dress of yours is going to look so pretty, ripped to tiny smithereens on my red satin sheets.'

The voice disappeared from her head and panic increased tenfold. If she had been sprinting before, now she was racing and thoughts tumbled around her head, disorganised and jumpy. It was a small consolation, but Violetta guessed she could be thankful for that. Martinet wasn't going to be able to read anything too coherent inside there for a while.

It took over a kilometre of fast running before she managed to calm herself down and get her bearings. Taking care not to divulge any landmarks, she concentrated on nothing more than Rafael's face as her feet hit the smooth pavement beside the Grand Canal. Sparkling glass shop fronts blurred before her eyes, decked out in pretty, bright coloured awnings, and there were padded chairs littering the pavement in a state of disarray where earlier 'al fresco' diners had left them. Looking up, the buildings began to tier in three and four stories, decorated with stone and black cast-iron balconies that would worship the sun come morning. She wondered if she would ever see the sun again. The thought was sobering. Her feet increased their pace but her lungs were tired, so damn tired. When the Rialto Bridge loomed up in the distance, graceful and elegant, with its presence providing a way to cross the expanse of water and enable her to reach her destination, she nearly sobbed in gratitude.

Crossing the four hundred year old footbridge might have been a problem during daylight hours, when swarms of tourists would make the ornate stone structure virtually impassable, but thankfully at this late hour there were no more than a couple of lovers decorating its yellowing balustrades. Her legs felt like lead, her left arm was pleading for mercy, and it felt like an inferno of fire had engulfed it. The pain was indescribable, but her feet continued to surge forward.

The vamp continued to keep a firm presence inside her head, taunting and tormenting her at every opportunity. At first, when her arm had been manageable, she had kept all details of her whereabouts firmly out of her thoughts, but with each new lurch of her foot that became impossible. She could think of nothing bar stopping the pain and she knew that was a weakness she couldn't afford to give in to. Her life depended upon her continuing forward.

She was no longer running. There was little she could do about it. Her feet had slowed to a painful crawl and her body was not functioning as it should. Dizziness, fatigue and shock were beginning to take their toll on her. There was no other option but to plough on forward though, so she gritted her teeth and ignored the provoking comments that frequently flew her way and tried to shut out her surroundings, wanting to give him no clues as to her final destination.

Bouncing off the walls of a narrow alleyway that could barely accommodate one person at a time, Violetta used both hands against the cold stone to push herself onward. Boutique hotels, pizzerias and quaint little shops selling all manner of Venetian coloured glass and trinkets hit the back of her retina, but did not make it into her thoughts. It was the only defence she had left against him, and considering the state of her head at this moment in time, it was an impressive enough feat in itself. She hobbled along as best she could and when finally the tall, pyramidal spire of St Mark's Bell Tower came into view, her relief was palpable. A tall and imposing structure, it loomed high above Venice and was a beacon to tourists and locals alike. At this precise moment in time it could have been an angel, much like the delicate wind vane in the form of Archangel Gabriel that decorated its tip, although it was not visible to her in the night sky. Just a few more metres, she pleaded with her legs, and the angel must have heard her, for the close proximity of the basilica spurred her on from a crippling walk to a slow and laboured jog. At least it was an improvement of sorts.

When she finally rounded the bend and found herself in the Piazza St Marco, if she'd had an ounce of air left in her body she would have breathed a sigh of relief. Salvation was just a few small steps away.

The wittering inside her head continued and one particular little shot struck her right where it hurt.

'You will be trained in the arts of pleasure, obedience and servitude. You will excel at them all, and when I get bored of tasting the delicious vintage that flows throughout your body, I will change you and then your torment will really begin. Will you fight me, Violetta?'

She wasn't able to prevent her immediate response of, 'Every step of the damn way.' She cursed herself inwardly for reacting to his words, hoping he could not trace her through them, but she couldn't think straight at this moment in time. The only thing on her mind was the desperate desire to reach her goal before he was able to manifest himself in front of her. As the five arched portals of St Mark's Basilica rose majestically before her, Violetta drew her head aloft and wanted to weep. Dragging her body onward, fuelled by nothing more than the desire to see another sunrise, she knew she had a chance. One single chance at survival.

The Basilica

A forest of columns and patterned marble slabs flew past. She didn't give them a second glance. Her slow jog had managed to increase in pace to a run. With only moments before The Winged Lion, which hung above the entrance to the Basilica, came into view she could afford to splurge on the last vestiges of her energy. Above her were the beautiful upper level mosaics depicting the life of Christ, and then came the four bronze horses of St Mark. She had reached her destination. Flinging herself up the stone steps and banging on the door hysterically, she could only hope there would be someone to receive her at this hour.

The door opened silently and she was greeted by the dim interior within, lit by little more than candles and a few strategically placed bulbs, but oh, how they reflected the light. Rushing inside her sanctum and striding forward, as if being further inside the church would help in her plight for safety, she couldn't help but be stunned by the richness of its design. There was a reason it had been given the nickname of Chiesa d'Oro, or Church of Gold. Glittering mosaics lined both the floor and the ceiling, and the gold glass created a shimmering movement that was truly incredible. Looking up into the vast height between herself and the domed ceiling, she had reason to feel very small. Then something clicked inside her and she realised that not only had she not seen a priest at the door, but no one had made a sound since her entrance. Spinning around to scan the area behind her, she saw that while the door had been closed firmly shut there appeared to be not a soul in sight. Whilst Violetta would normally have been more than capable of taking care of herself, she was in no fit state to defend herself this evening. She could only hope that the benevolent priest who had answered her call had left her some privacy in which to pray.

'My, what an impressive effort, chérie. Futile, of course, but impressive nevertheless.' Jumping up in shock she looked around and searched frantically for a member of the clergy to come to her rescue. There was no one to be found. 'The priests have been disposed of, chérie. It's just you and me.' And there he was, pristine perfection, looking cool, calm and unruffled. His full-length dark-grey coat had not a mark upon it, his loafers were polished to a high shine and his hair flopped in beautiful ebony planes against his face. Not even the wind was able to mar his beauty. He was lounging against a sixteenth century font to her left and looked exceptionally comfortable there. She wanted to burst into tears.

Speechless, she watched as both his hands cupped together and gathered water from the font. He liberally splashed himself with it and she knew he wanted a reaction from her. Goddamn, the man was an utter bastard. She refused to give him one. Violetta Cancellaro was not going to run over to him and try to tear his eyes out of his head. That would give him exactly what he wanted. She could not school her expression, however.

Her mouth dropped open in dismay. 'You,' she accused, though no further words were forthcoming. Her hands were shaking at the thought of what he might have done to the priests. If she had not come here tonight they might still be alive. She had an awful moment where she wondered how many deaths would be heaped upon her conscience. 'Why did you have to kill them?' Her legs crumpled and her knees sank to the tessellated carpet of marble below. They hit the cold, unforgiving floor with a dull thud.

'Oh yea of little faith,' he mocked. 'Contrary to popular belief, I do not go around murdering messengers of God or deflowering virgins on a regular basis. For you I'll make a special exception, but the general rule is to steer well clear of them.' He raised an eyebrow at her, knowing full well that she did not believe him. 'Relax, chérie. I sent them to sleep. They are having a quiet snooze up near the altar.'

She immediately scrabbled to her feet and turned around to confirm his words. On closer inspection she found two figures, both clad in voluminous black cassocks, could be seen strung across the front pew. A few halting steps forward, and she could see that he had in fact told the truth, for both chests were rising and falling and the sound of gentle snores could be heard. She remembered to breathe.

'Come now, princess. It's time to take a little trip. I have a four-poster bed and several sets of handcuffs with your name on them, although I think that the dark black rope would look particularly fetching wrapped around your alabaster arms. What do you think, darling?'

She thought, with a growing sense of fatality, that there was no way she was going to win this fight. He had her figured out every damn step of the way. If this were a game of chess it would be checkmate. 'We are not going to...' Violetta searched around desperately for the word to describe what they might do together... in his bedroom. 'Make love,' she squeaked. Although she already knew, without a doubt, that the expression was completely wrong. There was no love and not an ounce of kindness to be found anywhere in Monsieur Martinet.

His lips quirked. 'You are indeed correct, darling. We are not going to "make love".' He began walking towards her, laid-back strides, and his smile was that of a killer beast. 'We are going to fuck. Over and over again, until you get it just right, and then we are going to fuck some more. Perfection takes a lot of practice and I'm the kind of vamp that likes to get things just so.' He came within touching distance of her trembling body and reached out, beckoning her forward.

'Why aren't you dead?' Turning her head swiftly, making sure she did not look upon his beautiful face, she let anger flow hotly through her veins. Why couldn't this dreadful beast be stopped? Was he truly immortal? If that were the case she was already damned to eternity and the hell beyond.

'Give me your hand, precious.' He reached out five elegantly long fingers and beckoned her forward to emphasize his point. She stared at him, horror-struck and appalled.

'You are so pathetically easy to read, darling, it's almost laughable. 'You can't escape me. Deep down, you know that. You can fight me, but you also know I'd enjoy that. If you give me any trouble I'll simply knock you out.' He raised his eyebrows and looked at her intently. 'Would you prefer that? Not knowing what might happen to that amazingly beautiful body of yours, while your mind is hidden away in the depths of unconsciousness?' The last sentence was whispered in her ear as his hand snaked out to grab her wrist and pull her sharply into him. He ran his hand over her naked buttocks, caressing the belt lines from earlier, and then pressed down upon them. Violetta couldn't help a bleat of complaint. They stung like fire.

'Mmm. You'll feel those, and the latter ones I'm going to give you tomorrow for a couple of days. Will you earn yourself any more this week, I wonder?' He gave her rounded butt cheek a swift nip and was entertained when she spun around to face him with rage burning through her violet eyes. 'How does it feel to be parading yourself around the streets of Venice with no panties?' His hand leisurely explored the globes of her ass before he let a single finger dip to the valley between them. He ran it slowly downward and noted her very visible trembling. 'Quite decadent, I suspect.' His finger slid to her sex and dipped inside to test the waters. She squeaked in mortification and tried to pull away, but his immoveable grip held her fast. 'I don't think I will allow you to wear panties ever again, princess, although that may not be saying much as your lifespan could be likened to a ticking time-bomb.' His finger, now generously lubricated, circled the tight little hole of her sphincter, and twist as she might she could not escape it. 'You'll certainly have to be on your best behaviour, I fear. If you annoy me I'll probably kill you. If your performance upsets me I'll kill you. If you bore me I'll most certainly kill you. I'd say the odds of a long and eventful life are looking less than favourable.' The tip of his finger burrowed inside her, though not where she expected, and she squawked in alarm, wriggling like mad to try and avoid his explorations.

'You can't do this here,' she mumbled in shock, feeling his finger work its way inside her, unsure as to whether she wanted to slap him or fall into a puddle of desire at his feet. She needed to concentrate, but her body had turned into a pile of uncoordinated mush.

'Oh, I believe I already am, chérie. I can do anything I like, anywhere and with anyone I choose. Pulling the hard point of a nipple that had been taunting him through the sheer outline of her dress, he laughed as another pitiful squeak left her lips.

'Why aren't you dead?' She repeated her sentence slowly and purposefully. Her jaw was set tightly and her eyebrows were trying to form a deep 'V' of consternation.

'Chérie, chérie,' he purred, with his beautiful French accent, rolling the r's with impossible skill, 'I thought we'd covered this. I am unstoppable, unbeatable, unscrupulous and completely unethical. You do not stand a chance. Churches will not destroy my hardened flesh, knifes will not pierce it. Stakes will not find their mark and even the most beautiful of huntresses will not be able to crack the impenetrable shell that has encased my body. Face facts: you are mine, or to be more precise, your body is mine.' He pulled his finger out of her incredibly wet hole and moved back underneath her dress to give her bottom a swift smack. 'And I intend to utilise every inch of it to my absolute satisfaction. I will have my revenge, princess. You have no idea what I have in store for you, and that's probably for the best. If you did, I'd wager you'd kill yourself now.' Clearing his throat he ran his wet finger along his bottom lip and sucked upon it. 'Delicious.' His blue eyes clouded over in front of her and she knew that whatever was about to come out of his mouth would not be good.

'Envision yourself tied to my bed, sliding about on my red satin sheets - completely naked bar the soft black ropes that would enfold your wrists and ankles in its firm embrace. I would feed you, bathe you, and see to every single one of your needs, bar the most important, perhaps. For I intend to create a raging desire within that perfect body of yours that will swiftly give you a thirst for pleasure that is unquenchable. My hands will familiarise themselves with your beautiful curves, my lips will kiss every exposed inch of flesh and my body is going to torment yours in ways you could never imagine. Yes, that will be a fitting start to your stay, but there will be plenty of work ahead of us. Those delectable heart-shaped lips of yours will be trained to utter the dirtiest of words, your stamina will have to improve if you're having sex several times daily with a vampire, and you'll need to be taught technique. I'm a hard taskmaster. I think obedience training is where we will have the most difficulties, but we will get there in the end, chérie.'

His smug, self-satisfied demeanour and the careless lilt of his words had her reeling. Violetta could stand no more of it. The moment his fingers removed themselves from her body and all stimulation stopped was awful. The pleasure he had bestowed upon her had taken the edge off her broken shoulder, but now she had recovered her wits it made itself known again and the agony was incomparable to anything she had felt before. This evening had easily been the worst night of her entire life, but she refused to give him her body on a platter and he should know he wasn't getting a free meal. Even though the pain that coursed through her was debilitating in the extreme and now encircled her entire body, she wrenched herself up to full height and looked Martinet square in the eye.

She spoke clearly and enunciated each of her frigid words very carefully. 'If I'm going down, I'm taking you with me.' As she said her sentence she felt her head swim with the glimmering gold of the Basilica. The light bounced off her retinas and refracted into a thousand tiny beams inside her head. Blinking stupidly she tried to focus, but her eyes swam in the blurry lines of double vision. She was going to faint and there was little she could do about it. She hadn't drunk or eaten a thing in hours, had suffered a stress overload, and had also managed to break her shoulder, all in the space of a few hours. Her body was about to shut itself down. The thought was unbearable. Would he kill her? Would he kidnap her? Endless possibilities of nastiness fluttered through her head before the bliss of blackness came down all around her in a suffocating net. There was nothing she could do to save herself. Her life was in the hands of a monster. As her skull went flying towards the marble mosaic of the Basilica floor she couldn't utter a single sound.

'You can try,' was the ominous reply to her earlier question, and that was the last thing she heard. The lights had gone out.

Martinet caught her just before her head hit the undulating journey of a myriad of mosaic tiles. Her hair dusted the floor and her arms flopped out at an awkward angle, but no further damage was done to her body. His, however, was not in such great shape.

The garlic oil had burned simmering welts into the flesh of his lower legs and they throbbed and pounded through every pore of his being. He desperately needed fresh blood. His injury had sharpened his hunger even further and now the slow, dragging pulse that ran through Violetta's body was pure torture. He knew he could not drink from her in the state she was in. It added to his torment. Her smell was intoxicating in the extreme, and if he took her vein now he wouldn't have the necessary willpower to stop before he extinguished her life. That couldn't happen. It would be far too quick and painless. If he was to get any peace in the barren, endless life she had left him with, his huntress would need to pay for the deaths of his family. If he somehow managed to avenge their murders there was a chance that he might manage to make it through his eternal hell with his mind intact. If he were to become a raving lunatic, and there was a distinct possibility that he might, the omnipotent, preternatural being he had become would wreak havoc upon the world of man, and it wouldn't be pretty. He had been responsible for more than enough carnage in his youth and he had no wish to repeat the experience. He needed to find some kind of solace within himself, and at the moment she was the only plausible answer.

Flinging her over his shoulder, grateful that the oil had only affected the lower half of his body, he strode forth from the hallowed halls of the Basilica. The cloying scent of incense and candlewax filled the air, and although he had a great respect for buildings as exuberant and exotic as this, he would be glad to escape its opulent, dizzying confines.

Whilst on the subject of dizziness, he had counted on her fainting, and thankfully she had obliged him. With his hunger so acute and his legs feeling as if they'd been stung by a box jellyfish he would have been in no state to chase her around Venice, and putting her in a trance would have required more energy than he had available right now. His body was suffering from hypotension. Trying to repair the damage she had wrought with her holy water, he required more blood than was currently available. Nausea rolled off him in waves, violent muscle cramps rippled all over, and he was more than a little unsteady on his feet.

He could only be thankful he had seen fit to place a drop of venom within her body before he let her run. Oh, he knew she had been headed to the Basilica, on that score he had read her like a book. He hadn't needed to rummage inside her head for that little detail, and while it had been a slow and painful stroll for him, he had still managed to enter a good ten minutes before her feet passed underneath St Mark and his band of angels. Long before she had graced the threshold of the cathedral he had spirited himself away in a small alcove to await her arrival.

Keeping a firm presence inside her head as she made a beeline for her destination, he had concentrated on getting her adrenaline level high and forcing her to run as fast as she was able. With the injury she had sustained her body would be weak and the additional fatigue of running would push her to the edge. As soon as the 'fight or flight' hormone had left her, the shock of what had happened had sunk in and her blood pressure hit the floor, much the same as his. The difference was he could still function under the hardship.

Hitting the deserted streets outside he forced himself to walk as fast as he was able. Normally the dead weight upon his back wouldn't even have registered as an encumbrance, but today his body suffered and throbbed under the ordeal. He didn't let it bother him. She was far too precious a cargo to consider leaving unattended somewhere. She was also far too beautiful. It was still somewhat unbelievable to think that she remained a virgin. It was something she would not remain for much longer. The thought kept his legs moving.

Throwing his head back to admire the sheet of sparkling diamonds in the night sky, he sighed to himself. His objective had been captured and rendered ineffective. Tick. Alas, the night had only just begun and there was lots to do. He needed to get her back to Oscura Dimora before sunrise and his usual methods of travel were unavailable to him, due to his 'low power' mode. This meant he had to go with the standard 'old-fashioned' version, which in his book equalled a car, albeit a top of the range German one. He pulled his cell-phone out of his pocket and spoke the single word 'Luca' into it. A rapid chorus of speed dial bleeps took care of the rest.

'Get me the car. Bring it around to Piazzale Roma and make sure the tank's topped up. Be with you in thirty minutes or less. Thank you.' Sliding the cell-phone back into his pocket he frowned. That was one problem easily taken care of. Now, how was he going to get an unconscious girl all the way across Venice without being set upon at every turn? The answer, of course, was exceptionally easy: a gondola. There were hundreds of the things everywhere.

Approaching the Venetian Lagoon, and thankful they were under the cover of darkness, with the streets lit up by nothing more than the beautiful three-tiered lamppost lanterns, he found a suitable vessel that looked seaworthy and, more importantly, he knew where the oar was kept. It was amazing how many secrets one could discover over the years. Now it was time to put his simple plan into action.

Lowering his load carefully within its confines, not wanting to place any further stress on her body, at least for the time being, he laid her down on her side and placed her arms in front of her head to stabilise her body. The water was relatively calm, but you never knew what you might meet on the canal at this hour. When satisfied she was relatively safe he applied himself to the task of crossing the breadth of Venice. Firstly he used his talons to tear the mooring lines to shreds. It was far easier than unravelling the cord and he was impatient. Standing tall, to the rear of the boat, he got to grips with the long wooden oar. Setting it in its oarlock, or forcola, as the Venetians called it, he began rowing with a forward stroke.

The simple action of rowing sent his mind back centuries. He could easily remember Venice during the hay-days of the gondola, where there might have been as many as ten thousand boats gracing the canals. That was way back in the seventeenth century. In current day Venice there were only about four or five hundred left in service, but on the plus side, there were no traffic jams.

It took a reasonable amount of skill and a good degree of balance to get the thing moving in a straight line, but this wasn't the first time he'd had the privilege of rowing one. Handling the rocking gondola with care as he initially pushed it away from its mooring, he soon got them moving with a long stroke and a smooth rhythm. The oar was heavy. It was a thirteen foot pole of solid beech, and whilst this normally wouldn't have been a problem, today his hands shook against it, even though he held it loosely. It couldn't be helped. Pulling the paddle back and letting it slice silently through the black water he headed for the Rio de San Zulan, which would cut through to the Grand Canal in relatively short order. He moved as fast as he could. He knew his strength was going to diminish rapidly as his body tackled the burns that littered his lower legs. Once they were in the car his lack of strength wouldn't be a problem. Thankfully it was an automatic and all he would need to do was sit and stare for just over two hours. Propelling a gondola was another matter entirely. It was hard work if the journey was anything over ten minutes, and theirs certainly would be.

The Bridge of Sighs sped behind them, spanning two buildings and stretching high above the canal. The sad and angry stone faces carved upon it stared into his back, but he didn't let it worry him overmuch. He could remember a time when convicted prisoners would be marched from the old prison in the Doge's Palace across to the new prison on the other side, and they were not happy times for all concerned. Executions at the hands of the inquisitors were messy, bloody and nasty affairs. Much like the deaths Violetta had lately favoured and which she had probably planned for him this evening, except she was now on the losing end of the equation. He watched the slow rise and fall of her chest as the gondola quietly threaded a path through the water, and wondered where his revenge would take him.

She had picked a bad time to try and kill him. At the moment he was still consumed by grief for Adelise, who had passed away exactly ninety-one days ago. The last of his family had died the most hideous and painful death at the hands of his huntress. From the deepest place imaginable he had grieved and it ravaged his body and mind to the point of madness before he managed to come out the other side. He had tried to let it go, let it pass through him so it would leave him intact if not insensible. She had been the last of his line and the oldest, bar him. When she died it felt as if something central to his being had been ripped away, never to return. He had lost a part of himself that day, something so intrinsic to his being that he would never be the same again. A cold carcass of a man remained, where before there had once been love and light. That would never return. No being on earth could give him back that. He would have walked into the light and killed himself seconds after her death had that been an option, but he had known. While he had tried to deny it, even to himself, he knew what kind of a beast he had become. He had been granted the ultimate gift of immortality and power, but for him the cost had been too high - far too high. He felt tears pool in his eyes and blinked them away. This was not the time or place for them. He had an agenda and come hell or high water, the chit would pay for what she had done to his family. The only question was, would he show her more mercy than she had shown the other members of his brethren? What would be a fitting course of revenge for the woman who had removed every single colour bar black and white from his life? Oh and red, of course. Every night he dreamt in varying shades of blood-soaked red.

Memories

By the time he managed to reach the Piazzale Roma the time was approaching two a.m. and the journey had taken longer than he'd anticipated. Though his body was now visibly quivering all over, he knew the worst was yet to come and he had not a moment to lose.

Thankful that the streets were virtually empty at this time of night, he slung his comatose prisoner over his back once again and hopped onto dry land. His legs were unsteady beneath him, but they were able to make the short walk to the Santa Chiara Hotel without giving way beneath him, even with the sack of potatoes on his back. Why, oh why hadn't he fed before this evening's proceedings? But he already knew the answer to that one. He would need to be on permanent guard around her, and that was always easier when there was hunger in his belly. A sated vampire was a sloppy one.

Spying the coach park beside the hotel he immediately headed towards it, which was where his Audi S8 had been parked. He always carried the key chip in his pocket and tonight was no exception, so all he had to do was place his finger upon the door handle, wait for the release click, and pull. He dumped her unceremoniously on the back seat, pulling her knees up to her chest, and breathed a sigh of relief. She would have to make do without a seatbelt, just this once. He wasn't sure he had the necessary energy or coordination in order to get her into one. His eyes zoomed in on her face and he bent down to check her pulse once more. His normally acute senses, which should have been able to read these things, were becoming more and more muddled with the loss of blood.

Reaching down he bent her neck gently to the side allowing him access to her carotid artery. He compressed it. A reedy, fluttery beat met the tips of his fingers and her face was deathly pale, but he suspected she'd make the drive up to the mountains in one piece. She had to. There was no other option. For the moment he needed her alive. His sanity depended on it. Slamming the rear door shut he moved to the front of the car. Sliding into the black Valcona leather seats, he fired the engine up and listened to the deep monotone roar as the car sprang to life. Hugging the steering wheel tightly he sat up straight and moved the gear selector lever to drive. It was time to hit the road.

The roads, much like the streets of Venice, were eerily quiet at this time of night. All he had to do was set the cruise control, sit back, and enjoy the ride. If that were at all possible in the state he was in, which it wasn't. To keep himself occupied on the long journey home, while the car's twenty inch alloy wheels ate up the motorway, he fiddled with numerous dials and switches until the radio came on. It wasn't long before he was in a world of his own. He always listened to classical music when driving. It relaxed him, and as of late life had been much more stressful than usual.

Beautiful strands of orchestral music soon began to weave in and out of the surround sound Bose speakers and they wrapped their calming influence around him. It helped. Little by little his grip upon the wheel lessened, although the shaking of his hands did not. And then Verdi's Messa da Requiem began to pour from the stereo and he was spirited far, far away, to a time and place where this mess had all begun.

It hit him then. Hard. He relived each of their deaths every day, one by one. Whilst he supposed he should have been grateful that their suffering had finally ended, his anger increased tenfold with each soul that departed from his grasp. These were his brethren, those who had stood by him in both good times and bad, some for many hundreds of years. The first death that Violetta had doled out to his youngest son was about to re-enact itself in his brain for the umpteenth time, and it was not going to be a pleasant affair. Rubbing a tired hand over his forehead, as if it would help erase the memory, he then banged his head against the seat rest, as if the action might prevent what was about to happen. It was wishful thinking. He'd never managed to escape one of his flashbacks, and tonight would not be any different.

Gilles had been handpicked for Violetta's first assignment, probably because he was the youngest and most inexperienced of all Martinet's children. He would have been the easiest target for a huntress earning her wings, and indeed he had been. The huntress had come at him with virtually no experience whatsoever and it should have been an easy win for the vampire, except for the fact that he had been actively seeking death for the better part of the last decade.

Gilles had been the sensitive one. He would look at you with soulful, caramel eyes and instantly know what you were thinking. That had been a human trait which became much more pronounced as he was turned. It made him an excellent companion, as he knew when to provide company and when to stay away. He always had just the right words to offer and the gentlest touch of his finely boned hands would provide comfort. It wasn't often you found that in a vampire. He could also keep his mind quiet, and for that alone Martinet had been eternally thankful. As head vampire his mind was always full of chatter and babble, and sometimes trying to concentrate on the simplest of tasks could become an impossible feat. All of his children had a constant presence inside his head and whilst he knew how to shut them out, it required plenty of energy and concentration that he didn't always want to expend. Gilles seemed to quiet the voices inside him, and lull them into submission, for a few minutes at least. It had made the weight of several hundred years of existence considerably lighter.

Violetta stalked him in the streets of Paris and he had made the job considerably easier for her by moving at the speed of a human, rather than using the impressive velocity he had been granted as a vampire. The man rarely used the preternatural traits he had acquired, unless they were for the benefit of others. It had been his trade-off; enabling him to cope with the new life he had been given.

He hadn't wanted to be turned, but Martinet refused to feel guilty for acting. Gilles had been condemned to death and was suffering with terminal cancer when they crossed paths. That was bad enough in itself, but made much worse by the fact that he was a doctor, and an oncologist to boot. He knew exactly what was coming for him and how the man hadn't gone crazy was anybody's guess. Stoically, he had worked up until he was barely strong enough to stand before taking to his bed. That had been Gilles all over; selfless to the core.

At first there had been a debt between the pair. The doctor had helped his family, having a background in Haematology and he'd kept their secret. He carried Martinet's venom, of course, so he could be checked upon at all times, but he never betrayed their kind. Quite the opposite, in fact, because he actively tried to help them with his research and though nothing conclusive had ever been found, the debt remained. Gilles had been one of the good guys and Martinet would have protected him with his life. The trouble was, his life was of no use to him. The disease ate away at his body with an appetite for destruction that was unstoppable and no matter how many specialists Martinet bankrolled or how much money he threw at the problem, a problem it still remained. Death had come for him and there were only two answers to that equation.

When Gilles had long since given up the pretence of eating, Martinet ensured that a nurse was there at all times to make him as comfortable as possible. There had been no visitors and he had no family to speak of, so the evenings had been Martinet's alone. Keeping a vigil beside the dying man's bedside, he had sworn not to interfere with the last days of the doctor's life. Gilles wouldn't have let him in the house under any other terms, not that he could have physically stopped him. Given no choice but to succumb to a dying man's last wishes, Martinet had little option but to agree with his request. This he did willingly, but he hadn't counted on several things back then. He hadn't known that his affection for Gilles would increase exponentially every damn day, and he certainly hadn't reckoned on how much pain would be heaped upon a dying man's body or how long and drawn out his death might be. After thirty days of agonised suffering, something inside Martinet snapped. Unable to bear another minute of Gilles tormented cries he bit him, paying no heed to the man's pathetic attempts to stop him. It was his own mind he had been concerned about. If he let him die and slip away never to utter another sound again, he would have endured endless guilt. Rebirthing the man in the manner of a vampire gave him a chance at proving there was another way, a better way, for his friend to exist. It had been a risk worth taking.

Gilles had never forgiven him, of course. For the first few years of his new life he sought death with a vengeance, which had Martinet following him night and day. The amount of times he'd had to scrape the young vampire up off the floor, dust him down and smile politely whilst giving him the necessary blood and space to heal had been appalling, but it changed nothing. He would have done it all again for as little as just one extra day of his life.

If he'd known how short the vampire's life was destined to be he might have rethought his actions, but it was far too late for recriminations now. Martinet had rebirthed a gentle and honourable man into a vampire, sparing him one awful death only to deliver him swiftly into another. For Violetta's first assassination attempt had been a gruesome affair and, unfortunately, that was exactly where his mind was headed and there was no avoiding it.

He remembered the very first time he set his eyes on her. Gilles had been feasting in one of his favourite brasserie's in Paris, bemoaning the fact that the exquisite French food he'd just eaten had been worse than tasteless in his mouth. He still could not get over the idea that the only sustenance he would ever find truly appetising was the fine vintage of freshly decanted blood. It amused Martinet no end. In the first few years of his life as a vampire, he trawled all over the world searching for the most renowned eateries and the most elegant dining establishments in the hopes that something would tempt his taste buds. A rare and bloody steak had been about the only thing he had enjoyed, and the pleasure derived from it was less than half of what it had been when he was human. He was not to be discouraged in his search though, and Paris remained his favourite haunt for gourmet fair. If he was not destined to enjoy it, he had decided he could at least admire the artful presentations that appeared on his plate, and the wine wasn't so bad either.

The huntress had sat at a table opposite him. He thought she had been waiting for her date and immediately felt sorry for her. Martinet remembered him thinking, 'The stupidity of man knows no bounds.' He had admired her discreetly, when he could tear his eyes away from his plate, and even though women were not his first choice for sexual partners, he had felt the sway her body held over his. Gilles had found it disturbing. Her beautiful fiery waves had been arranged in an elegantly long ponytail and tied back with a gold barrette at the nape of her neck. Her eyes had been smouldering under the weight of eyeliner and mascara heaped upon them, and those violet irises... when he'd caught her gaze accidentally he wanted to open his mouth in awe. She had been so disturbingly beautiful that he quickly finished his half-hearted attempt at eating and, flinging his napkin down in dismay, rushed from the restaurant to re-evaluate his sexual preferences.

That had been partly Martinet's fault. Although Gilles was unaware of it, he was able to feel the emotions of his master if they were left unchecked. They rarely were. Martinet could disguise nearly all his reactions through many years of careful practice. Sexual chemistry such as that Violetta provided couldn't be masked on a moment's notice. It was something that happened far too rarely. A raging torrent of desire had hit him upside the head, and it wouldn't have hurt more had a hammer been raining down blows upon him. His chest had just discovered a weight that truly hurt, yet was lighter than air. Her presence immediately wrapped itself inside his body, and it felt like liquid fire running through his veins. Goosebumps erupted over his skin, which was crazy considering he was nowhere near her. What the hell had just happened?

Keeping himself a firm but silent presence inside Gilles' head, he had tried to search for her to no avail. Gilles was walking fast and purposefully kept his head low. All Martinet managed to get was a detailed view of the concrete pavement and it was more than a little frustrating. He couldn't very well order Gilles to look around, because that would indicate his interest in little Miss Redhead, and he hardly wanted to declare it to the world at large. He would have to bide his time and wait and see if she crossed his path again.

The wait, as it happened, was a lot shorter than he had anticipated.

Gilles had been headed home to the attic apartment in Saint Germain-des-Prés. Martinet had owned it for more than three hundred years, and its value was now astronomically ridiculous. The neighbourhood had been home to all sorts of famous personages, such as Pablo Picasso and Oscar Wilde, and the characterful streets and expensive designer boutiques had provided much amusement for his family over the years.

Punching in the entry code, Gilles wrapped his beige Mac high around his ears to keep out the chill wind of a December night and his brow wore a furrowed frown. He was annoyed that he couldn't get the startlingly clear image of the redhead out of his mind. Her violet eyes were still burning into the back of his retinas. A sliver of unease overtook his body. An older vampire would have recognised it for what it was: a warning. Gilles put it down to the lateness of the hour and thought no more of it.

Hearing the lock click he opened the tall white wooden door only to find a tendril of vividly bright auburn hair draped over his shoulder. He had turned around in shock, thinking he had been seeing things, and there was Violetta. The avenging angel had marched straight past him, the tails of her long red wool coat trailing behind her, and the scent of Chanel No. 5 wafted delicately in her wake. Gilles felt himself harden at nothing more than the view of her receding posterior. He almost swore out loud.

'Who are you?' He let the door behind him slam shut and stood still as a statue, silently assessing his uninvited guest. Curling both hands into fists he waited patiently for an answer. It was just as well he had all the time in the world, because she took an eternity to turn around. Martinet remembered that much very clearly, because he had been hungering after the slightest glimpse of her and time almost crept to a standstill as the first sight of elegant cheekbones came into view.

She began unbuttoning the large red buttons that decorated the length of her, from neck to mid-thigh. Shrugging out of the heavy coat she draped it over the side of an ancient Chesterfield sofa.

'I am your saviour,' she had said in English, and that was when Gilles knew he was in trouble. People from around these parts did not speak English; not if it could possibly be avoided, in any case.

'I am here to release you, Gilles. Release and liberate your soul.' She had drawn her knife dramatically. Back then she kept it in her pocket, but as the years had gone by the woman had learned from her mistakes, but that was another story entirely. Holding the knife aloft she let the blade twist in the dull lamplight of the quaint sitting room, so that its silver planes caught the light and gave notice of her intentions. He stared at her open-mouthed for a few seconds, and then he laughed.

'Oh Madame. You are late, so very late. I have been actively searching for death these past few years with little success. Well, that and a decent meal at any rate.' He held his hands out to his sides in a gesture of surrender, smiled and said, 'I'm all yours. Just make it quick.'

She took him at his word. Walking towards him she kept eye-contact, letting him admire her shapely curves and the bounce of her luscious red hair. When in touching distance she paused, almost as if she couldn't believe her luck, but Gilles remained where he stood, true to his word.

'Any last words?' Her voice was now a mere whisper of sound, but of course he heard it.

Gilles saw her throat swallow in panic, watched her wrist tremble around the knife's hilt, and heard the quiver in her voice. He was to be killed by a huntress, of that much he was sure, but he wondered if she would be capable of what she threatened. Her composure was now somewhat lacking. Trust his luck to get the newbie.

He grabbed a fistful of her hair and slid his hand around her neck, bringing her into his chest. He inhaled her scent and sighed mournfully. She could not move out of his grasp and he felt her struggle against him as the first whit of true panic took root. She would need to improve her game if she wanted to stay alive long in her line of business. He didn't feel charitable enough to tell her so, though.

Pushing her away from him he took a step back and cleared his throat. 'I'm sorry, Michel,' he murmured, 'but I cannot live the life you have forged for me. I hope you find another who can.' Having said his piece he simply nodded at her and waited. Thankfully the huntress did not dawdle in her plotted attempt on his life.

The knife arced in the air and plunged for his throat. It must have been honed to a fine edge for it sliced cleanly through several layers of skin and fat, and moved downward in a straight line, puncturing his lung. Gilles felt a whoosh of air leave his body and blood bubble up his throat. Though he did not need air, or the inflation and deflation of a pair of lungs to pump said substance around his body, he did need blood and he was losing it fast. Death could not come soon enough. He had begun to wonder if his time would ever come, but by the looks of it death had arrived, and by all that was holy it was the most beautiful thing he had ever seen.

Feeling his soul begin to detach itself away from his body, a strange light-headedness overcame him. Euphoria? It was an interesting enough thought. But there was no time for musings because his was not to be an easy death. He supposed he almost deserved that much, for Gilles had known what Michel would do to him, and had known that the life of a vampire was to be his. He also knew he would not be able to stop him, because he was aware of one thing that not even the vampire had realised back then. Michel Martinet had been in love.

Feeling his head sway as his life-force leaked from his body, he watched as she struggled with the dragging motion of the knife, aiming for his heart but not having the necessary strength to accomplish the feat. Placing her two hands on the hilt didn't accomplish the task either. She was such a slight thing, far too skinny for her own good. The girl needed a decent meal or two to fatten herself up. He almost laughed. His whole life had been a mess, why should his death be any different?

As the blade began to burn like fire he watched her joined hands wobble as the knife stilled, and for an awful moment he was afraid he might live through this. She was unable to go any further. 'Goddamn,' he had gurgled in a voice that was not his own, and somehow he added his hands to her blade and with one fearsome yank, his heart was sliced cleanly in two and it was over. It was all over.

Martinet had watched the light die in Gilles' eyes. When the Rembrandt on the wall shot upward and nothing but the fuzzy outline of wood floor and skirting boards filled his brother's eyes, he knew his time was almost over. He was helpless to lift a finger. Gilles was in Paris, he was in London. Vampires moved quickly, but not that quickly. His mind reeled. 'Stop the bleeding,' he had ordered, his voice harsh, uncontrolled panic taking over his body. Although the young vampire's hands sluggishly raised themselves to try and obey his Master, they never even made it halfway. Blackness engulfed Martinet's head. Blackness remained in the spot where the light and life of Gilles had been only moments before. He had thrown back his head and screamed. Hot tears poured down his face as grief consumed him. For one who prided himself on his lack of emotion, the loss of his son had produced a devastating misery that nothing could touch. But that was just the beginning of his family's life being shot to hell...

Finally the flashback ended and he was released from its powerful grasp. Switching off the radio, it was all he could do to stop the tears from pouring again. He needed to focus on the present. He had his objective and it was time for payback. He had waited an awfully long time to get even, and it was only fitting that he took his time in achieving his goal. Martinet suspected he had a lot of hard work ahead of him, but it wouldn't be all bad. She had a body to die for and the face of a beauty queen. However much he wanted to abhor her, the fact remained that he'd probably have to settle for intense dislike. He didn't have to like someone to enjoy fucking them though, so there might be a God after all. His train of thought abruptly ended as he hit a bump and the car went flying.

The top speed of the Audi was reported to be 155mph and when he looked down at the illuminated amber dial before him, it was to realise that the poor engine was almost at the limit of its endurance, and oh how he knew that feeling well. Taking his foot off the gas he slowed down on the approach as they rounded a hairpin bend that would have thrown most other vehicles off the road if they'd tried it at the breakneck pace he had used. Four wheels remained on the tarmac, thankfully, but his hands rattled against the steering wheel and it was now a struggle just to turn the damn thing. He had no choice but to plough on, deep into the mountains. There was no recourse for failure.

After another half an hour of driving and he sighed in relief as the enormous flat-topped monoliths of the Dolomite Mountains began to rise all around him. It was not before time. The vicious turns and twisting mountain passes had begun to take their toll on his arms, and he found them jerking and banging against the Audi's interior, almost uncontrollably. His legs were in a worse state, but thankfully they weren't needed as it wasn't a stick shift. As they began ascending into the mountain range, higher and higher with each kilometre that passed by, he felt his body weakening degree by degree. By the time they got to his little hideaway he'd be reduced to crawling. Still, it wasn't the first time he'd had to crawl as a vampire and it probably wouldn't be the last. Suck it up, he told himself, after his arm did a particularly vicious flip and slammed into the rear window behind him. Biting down on the groan of pain that wanted to escape, he rounded the final bend and let the car tear off down a rutted dirt path that would shortly take them to the entrance of his underground home. Surrounded by a tumbling hedgerow of weeds on either side, he forged a path through some of the more aggressive ones. The track was rarely used and left poorly maintained for a reason. It kept annoying tourists at bay.

They bounced around frantically for a few minutes, which was nothing Martinet hadn't been doing already, though it probably didn't do Violetta any favours in the back seat. She'd just have to hang in there for a moment. When the path finally broadened out they were met by an alpine log house that was typical of the South Tyrol region. White louvered shutters decorated the windows and a long wooden balcony ran around the middle of the house. This was decorated with a series of large terracotta tubs bearing all manner of bursting floral accomplishments. A copse of leafy beech and conifer trees encircled the property and disguised the sheer cliff-face only a few meagre yards behind it.

Martinet gave up a silent prayer of thanks and began to wrench the keys out of the ignition. Shutting off the engine he parked outside the villa and, with a struggle, managed to get himself outside the car on legs that could have belonged to a newborn giraffe. Still, it was better than crawling. As he fought to put one foot in front of the other he made his way shakily down the little lane that skirted the house, for that was not where he was headed. He was about to dive down the cliff-face, where the entrance of Oscura Dimora lay. It would be an interesting journey in his present condition, to say the least.

He did not spare a thought for Violetta. The villa was empty and they were in the middle of nowhere. Even if someone had been about they'd be unlikely to go peering in strange cars at this time of night, and as his had tinted windows, even if they did they wouldn't be able to see much. When you took into consideration that the car door would automatically lock itself when the key fob was a couple of metres out of reach, she was pretty safe and he had to be content with that. He'd come back for her as soon as he was able.

Martinet usually enjoyed the scramble down the limestone cliff, which on a normal day would have taken him barely a minute or two. Alas, things were not going to be that straightforward today. His body was jerking uncontrollably at every opportunity and his vampiric strength was non-existent. This was going to be messy and it was going to hurt. On the plus side, he was no stranger to pain and it certainly wouldn't hurt as much as the holy water incident. Trying his hardest to think up strategies that wouldn't involve the near loss of a limb, he debated the options before him.

Option one: dive down the cliff headfirst, hope to land somewhere close to the opening portal of his cave and scramble as best as he was able to the entrance.

Option one was not particularly inspiring. It would most definitely involve several broken bones, more bleeding and lots of swearing.

Option two: find some pitons, a couple of karabiners, some pulleys and then abseil down the mountain.

Option two was great, but he had none of the required items and doubted he could get his hands on the stuff at short notice. If he did, he suspected there'd be humans about and then he'd probably get distracted for quite some time.

Option three: find a reel of rope, tie it to something sturdy, hurtle down the cliff and improvise or swear where necessary.

Option three was the most realistic of the lot, and he was fairly confident there was some rope stored in the out-shed of the villa, which was always kept unlocked and should be relatively easy to retrieve. In just a few minutes he had done exactly that and in his hands he cradled some white nylon rope, one end of which he had somehow managed to tie around his waist and the other was fastened around the cast-iron latch handle of the shed door. He really hoped someone had screwed the thing on firmly, because if they hadn't he was shortly going to find it hurtling down the cliff towards him. It would have been sensible to tie it to something a little more sturdy, like the Audi perhaps, but he liked to live life on the edge; quite literally as it happened.

Walking slowly to the ledge before him he tested the messy double knot around his waist, and was less than impressed with the security it provided. Oh well. Looking down at the black pit of what was unmistakeably very hard rock below he grimaced, sucked in his cheeks and then jumped.

Oscura Dimora

Without a single thought of misgiving, Martinet leapt backwards off the cliff. That was one of the advantages, if you could call it that, of being a vampire. Death wasn't particularly scary. Yes, broken bones were an inconvenience, blood was a highly desirable commodity to be kept inside the body at all times and flesh still stung when scraped and bruised, but overall his body healed itself within minutes rather than days when these kinds of events struck. That still didn't mean he liked getting hurt in any way, shape or form, but as the years went by his pain tolerance seemed to increase with them. That was probably a good thing, because he had a bad feeling about this.

The first part of the jump went tolerably well. Air whistled up the length and breadth of him and chilled his skin to the bone, but the cliff stayed away from his body. This was good. He had allowed himself about two hundred metres of rope, because that was approximately where the entrance to his home lay down the cliff-face. Far enough down so that no enterprising tourists or rock climbers would manage to make it without one hell of a struggle, but not too far that it would be a tedious journey for himself every evening. All was going swimmingly until the makeshift bungee he had created for himself extended to its full reach. There was a sharp twang and an almighty force was exerted against his abdomen as the rope bounced back upwards towards the cliff. He'd expected that, and at this point things were still looking good. No nasty bumps, no rope burn, no broken ribs. So far this was a grand day out in his opinion, but it was not to last. When he began plummeting downwards again he caught a glimpse of the narrow opening to his underground cave. He was within perhaps six or seven metres of the thing and he tried to sway towards it when the rope reached the end of its limit once more. This time, when he waited for the bounce back up, it didn't happen. Martinet cursed a century's worth of hard-earned cuss words as his body began to plummet to the ground below.

The bloody handle did hit him on the head. He'd had a feeling it would, but he had no time to mourn his misfortune. The cliff-face was hurtling towards him at a rate of knots and if he didn't do something quickly it was going to give him a visage that would make Freddy Kruger look rather dishy. Alas his options were limited, so he got his talons out and turned his face to the side. There was a few seconds of nothing but pleasurable silence and then a sickening crunch as his body hit the wall of limestone rock at a velocity that sent several nasty cracks running through it. As his cheekbone smashed into the wall he had the foresight to angle his head back, but the damage had been done. His talons scraped anxiously for purchase, but did little more than rearrange some fallen scree before he began hurtling downward again, ready for round two. Martinet verses the wall. Geez, this was a fun game.

The second time he bounced into the cliff he was ready for it. The same cheekbone slammed against it, because he saw no point breaking two of the things, and his talons sunk painfully deep into the rock. The noise of them could be likened to someone scraping chalk against a blackboard, but he used considerably more force. The good news was he was now stationary. The bad news was he was halfway up a mountain with a sheer drop both above and below him - that and the possibility that his manicurist might never speak to him again. Still, he guessed he could be grateful he'd worn rubber-soled shoes this evening. They were going to come in handy. Placing them both flat against the cliff, he began scrambling upward.

Adrenaline and pain focused him as nothing else could, and after about ten minutes of scrabbling, clawing and swearing, he found the entrance to his cave. He flopped down, absolutely exhausted, on the narrow ledge that led into a small tunnel that burrowed steeply into the mountainside. He would need to give himself a couple of seconds before he attempted that, but the knowledge that fresh blood was only a few metres away would shortly spur him on. He could almost smell the stuff.

Laying his broken cheek down on the cold surface on the stone helped to numb and soothe away the pain. To be honest, he hardly even felt it. Today he was euphoric. Not only had he achieved his objective and captured his huntress with his life intact, but he was within hours of being able to play the most intense game of cat and mouse that was possible between a beauty and a beast. He wasn't exactly sure whom he would cast for each role, but he suspected time would tell. It always did. Get up, Martinet. Get up off the damn floor and get her inside somewhere safe.

It was an odd sentiment, considering he was planning to kill her, but it was instinctive. She was human and he still thought of her as fragile, though she had proved on more than one occasion this evening that she had a will of iron and nerves of steel. He would have to see what could be done about that. He needed to intimidate the girl and quickly. It would take around a week, give or take a few days, he guessed. After that she'd be careful to do exactly as he said, but he'd always have to maintain a firm presence within her head. If he ever made the mistake of underestimating her, he'd be dead. There was always at least one way to kill a vampire.

Get up. Get up now. He struggled to his knees, but did not have the necessary strength to make it to his feet. Goddamn. Another curse left his lips. Fine, he would crawl. Gritting his teeth he decided the huntress had won this round, but she wouldn't win the next. No, the next round would involve *her* crawling. There would be lots of crawling and she would be naked, pleading and begging for the release he would not grant her. She was going to get rather good at crawling by the time he'd finished with her.

He got halfway down the tunnel on all fours before he began seeing stars. There was hardly any blood left in him and his body was going into hypovolemic shock. His circulation was shot to hell. He had a paralysing moment when he wondered if he'd actually make it down the last few steps and into the kitchen, the first room in his oddly situated house and a wholly unnecessary one, bar the fridge. He'd kept a kitchen purely for Gilles and every time he saw the thing now he wanted to scream and shout out his loss. Fortunately, no one bar the servants would hear him down here. His master was long gone. There was a niggling worry in the back of his head that once he started the wailing and keening he might never stop. He had bottled up more grief than anyone should ever have to deal with in a lifetime, and he was at a loss as to how to deal with the stuff, bar his plans for Violetta. He guessed it would be a start. Keep moving. He was falling apart. The whole of him trembled like a Massai warrior who'd decided to take a vacation in the Arctic Circle. He was cold, so damn cold. Another inch. His hands scraped pitifully against the smooth stone steps and, using the last remnants of his energy he pushed himself forward, hoping to fall down the last ten or so stairs to the bottom.

His body lumped, bounced, scuffed and banged against each individual step, but he made it in one piece. He profusely thanked whichever servant had the foresight to place the modern stainless steel fridge at the entrance to the kitchen, even though he had just clunked his head on it, because with a single agonising wrench he had the door open and there in front of him were over a hundred clear plastic packets of blood. There were no niceties today. He ripped the top off the nearest bag and with badly shaking hands, threw the stuff all over him. Hopefully some of it would land in his mouth, and it would give him the strength to reach for another.

The time it took to go from weaker than a baby to strong as an ox was barely twenty minutes. Six bags of blood, twenty-five swear words and a whole lot of laundry later, Martinet was in the shower cleaning himself up. His lower legs still stung, but they'd already shown great improvement after the massive blood intake, and given another day they'd be right as rain. His cheek had swelled rather nastily and was still sore to the touch, but the bones had already knitted together and in a couple of days there wouldn't be a mark upon him. His huntress, however, would be bearing lots of marks. His. It was time to go and retrieve her.

He dressed all in black. It matched his mood. From the neatly pressed slacks to the thick cashmere roll-neck jumper that fit against his torso with exacting precision, he was ready and eager to start the night's proceedings. On feet that were now lighter than air he raced back up the steps and almost floated up the cliff-face. He felt good. His body needed to heal a little, but his strength had returned in full measure. There was a lot to be said for that. After several thousand years you became used to having extraordinary strength and out of all of his many talents, strength was one of the ones he appreciated the most. When it went it was sorely missed. He made the journey back to the car in less than five minutes, almost letting his enthusiasm get the better of him. Pausing, his hand on the shiny black door handle, he contemplated what he was about to do. Would he be able to live with himself after this? She was an innocent, she was young and he planned on taking her life. Could he cope with the guilt? He pursed his lips together and slowly ran his thumb across his mouth as he considered his next steps. Gilles' face floated before his eyes and then several others came up to join him. He shook his head. Hell yes, he could live with himself, and not only that, he'd damn well dance on her grave. If she could live with herself after all the cruelties she'd delivered in her incredibly small lifespan, then he should have no problems.

Pulling the door open sharply he picked her up carefully, supporting her neck in one hand and the curve just below her ass in the other. He cradled her to his chest and inhaled her. He sucked in a slow lungful of air and savoured her flowery fragrance. Lily of the valley. That's what it was. From the moment she'd first stepped in the ballroom he had singled out her very distinctive perfume but the particular brand she wore had remained elusive. It had niggled him. Over the years he had committed hundreds of bottles of scent to memory and had an especial fondness for Chanel, but Violetta had chosen something much less sophisticated and yet, the beautiful pure cut of the scent was far more intoxicating to him. If he wasn't much mistaken, she wore Penhaligon's Lily of the Valley and on her skin the smell was sublime. He closed his eyes and enjoyed the sensory overload for a moment. He would have to get her a bottle. The tantalising aroma did funny things to his insides, and he liked to encourage that at every opportunity.

'Wake up,' he whispered in her ear. He didn't really want to wake her, but the journey down the mountainside wasn't going to be pretty if he didn't get a little help.

'Where am I... what...?' her eyes were dazed, her tongue was thick in her mouth and her faced was pinched. Her arm. He'd forgotten about that, damn it. Burrowing inside her head he swiftly numbed the area. He was rewarded with a shaky smile. The girl must be dreaming. She'd be busy trying to claw out his vital organs otherwise.

'Hold onto my neck and shut your eyes.' The whisper was inside her head this time.

She gave him several confused, sleep-filled blinks of her eyelashes, so he repeated the command, giving her a little push. Obediently her arms snaked up around his neck, her fingers entwining tightly as her eyes fluttered closed.

And so they flew down the mountainside in a series of grand jumps, before he landed expertly on the small ledge that would lead to her new home. She would be spending her foreseeable future there, be that long or short. He didn't particularly care at this moment in time. He had designs on her body for the next week or two, and after that, they'd see. She deserved no promises. After he'd seen to her arm and the limb had repaired itself, he'd extract his revenge and enjoy every second of her torment. He fully intended to put her through hell and back. It was the very least she deserved, but it was all he was capable of, so it would have to do.

Walking down the same steps that had nearly been his undoing only minutes ago, he danced upon his toes and twirled his prize around in his arms. Her eyes snapped open at the dizzying movement. Large and voluminous in her beautiful oval face, they stared up at him with dawning comprehension. There was no fear, though there would be in the days to come. He'd make sure of it. Right now, it was a look of contempt and loathing that broadcast itself loud and clear without the need for words to be aired.

'Yes. You're doomed, princess. Get used to the idea.'

She did not give him the satisfaction of a response, merely closed her eyes and tried to shut him out. He laughed. 'That's hardly going to be very effective, darling. Not when I can easily rummage around in that delightful mind of yours.' He heard the scream of rage she stifled. He felt the tightening of her fists and her frustration at being so easily captured.

Manoeuvring her easily through the house, past the now spotless kitchen that housed little more than several pints of blood, he decided all that would have to change. If he wanted to keep her alive he'd need to feed her. A mug of sugary tea would probably keep her going until the morning when proper sustenance could be provided. The day he had planned was going to involve lots of exertions on her part, and she'd require plenty of energy.

Walking across the stone floor and nudging the oak panelled door of his bedroom open with his knee, he flung her across the room and watched as she landed bang in the middle of his bed. He watched her splutter and curse as she pulled herself up on his cherry-red satin sheets and finally she bit. 'Why don't you just kill me now and spare yourself the trouble of looking after me?'

It wasn't the words he had been expecting. 'So you admit you deserve to die?' He inclined his head in question and a fold of ebony hair slid across his cheek. Her heartbeat thumped erratically, and her body was drawn taut as a bowstring. He wondered if he might get an apology.

She gave him a derisive snort in response. 'Do your worst, Martinet. I have people who'll come for me. Just sleep with both of those wonderful blue eyes open, sweetheart, because I promise you that as soon as I find them closed, I'll rip them out.'

His lips narrowed and all at once pain flooded her body. He intensified the sensation so that she writhed about upon his bed in agony. His huntress was going to learn to keep her mouth shut unless she could find something nice to say. He watched her body coil in the throes of anguish for several long minutes before he said, 'It won't stop until you apologise.'

'Go. To. Hell.'

He admired her. He couldn't help himself. She'd never looked more beautiful, splayed out and thrashing her limbs around in a twisted mess across his bed. He desperately wanted to fuck her, but for that reason alone he'd make himself wait. He needed to tread cautiously around this one and she would require careful handling. He added another notch of nastiness that would have her endorphins screaming in no time. Another minute of thrashing ensued. Then a strangled voice could be heard.

'Please. Make. It. Stop.' Each word was bitten off and spluttered out whenever she had a chance to inhale a second's worth of air.

'Apologise.' He upped her level of torment again. To be honest, he was curious how much more the girl could take. She was much stronger than she looked. Finally a tortured scream left her lips.

'I'm sorry,' the words were gurgled and almost unintelligible, but it was a start and it would do.

'Apology accepted.' His steely glare descended upon her, sending slivers of metal deep into her spine, but he halted the pain instantly. Compliance was always rewarded. Walking slowly to the side of the bed, the sound of his footsteps echoing against the stone, his cool hand reached down to capture her wrist. She immediately pulled it away out of his reach.

A semblance of a smile began to twitch at the two corners of his lips. 'Do you realise how pointless that is? Do you really believe you can escape, outrun or outwit a vampire? His hand moved, so quickly that not even a blur was present in her vision. When she blinked the fingers of both his hands had surrounded her wrists and were digging tightly into the soft skin. When she wouldn't look him in the eye he simply commanded her head up and trapped her within his gaze. Two icy blue eyes bored into hers and the game for superiority was lost.

'Stay still. I'm going to fix that arm, unless you want to end up disfigured for life?' He raised an eyebrow at her. She didn't move, but neither did she give in gracefully.

'Why fix me? I'm here to be tortured, aren't I? That's what you want, isn't it? Revenge.' The violet petals of her eyes spat venomous fury. The woman looked so beautiful he wanted to paint and frame her.

'I'm going to fix you in order to break you properly. Breaking bones would be far too easy, Violetta. There are other torments that are far worse than physical trauma and pain. In order to experience them fully you need to be in the best of health, my dear. The good news is that with a few drops of my blood inside you, that shoulder will be good as new within a day. I just need to set it straight.'

When she struggled against him, as he knew she would, he paralysed her from the neck down. When she immediately started spluttering obscenities at him he wished he'd gone the whole hog and shut her down completely, but he needed to make sure he didn't make any mistakes and for that, he needed her conscious. If he made a mistake she wouldn't be. Ignoring the copious threats and curses directed his way, he let his mind tunnel into her body and spread itself carefully over the area that needed to be repaired. There was lots of damage to keep him occupied. A comminute fracture, the bone broken in several places, was going to take some careful healing. Add to that muscle, nerve and tissue damage and it was going to keep him busy for the better part of a half hour. He began the painstaking process of putting each piece of sinew and fibre back in its rightful place. Shutting out her entertaining, but rather distracting diatribe, he applied himself to the intricate process of mending the break. Knitting together bone fragments, tendons and ligaments, piece by tiny piece, required a great deal of concentration. It was such a mess the whole process took a little longer than he'd expected, nearly an hour in total, and at the end of his task he was spent. Violetta, on the other hand, had barely gotten started but he knew of something that would shut her up quickly.

His fangs, which had been threatening to burst from his lips the whole time he had been close to her, due to her unique and all-consuming smell, were finally allowed free rein. Bringing his forearm up to his lips he gently placed two puncture wounds in his flesh. His venom easily broke through the hard casing of his body and he felt his tongue lock as blood began to well to the surface of the twin holes.

He placed the droplets of blood in front of her lips for a second, purely to enjoy the look of horror that resided there. 'See? I don't have to break bones to torture and torment you. Tonight, Violetta, you shall drink blood. My blood, and it will be a sweet agony all of its own. But you'll find out why later. For now, drink and heal yourself, my sweet.' Her lips contorted instantly in repulsion, but he simply overrode her natural instincts and commanded her body to obey him. With her eyes wide with shock her lips descended and began to gently suck at the tiny glistening beads of burgundy fluid that he presented for her delectation.

Apparently the flavour was not to her taste, for she began to retch around his flesh, but he did not allow her the privilege of stopping. She needed to swallow at least a teaspoonful in order for his earlier work to be completed. Amidst several creative invectives he managed to discern that his blood was 'disgusting', with a 'rust or coppery' flavour. She couldn't quite decide which. Without a doubt she let him know that his particular taste was not to her liking. Too bad. She would drink until he told her to stop. Her face was a picture.

'That's enough.' He didn't need to pull her away, as he would have had to do with a fellow vampire. She immediately stopped as soon as his coercion had left her body. Finally the young woman was speechless, and not before time. She also looked exhausted. It had been a long day for a human, he supposed.

One of his servants walked in then, bearing a cup of English Earl Grey tea as he'd been ordered. Everything worked telepathically around here and pretty much flowed like clockwork. Knowing his master well, the servant carefully placed a bright flowery tray on the bedside table and departed as quickly and silently as he'd arrived.

Picking the fine gilt-edged bone china cup up, he blew gently on the wisps of steam that flowed upwards and cooled the boiling water down to a drinkable degree. Holding the cup of heavily-sweetened fragrant tea to her lips he said, 'Drink.' She had no choice but to obey his command and the fluid streamed down her throat and removed the earlier source of her discontent. He was such a thoughtful thing, really.

After she'd drained the entire contents, bar the last few dregs of murky tealeaves that sloshed about in a disorderly fashion at the bottom of the cup, he inclined his head slightly and asked, 'Better?'

Violetta looked at him very slowly through lidded eyes. She swallowed carefully and licked her lips, before clearing her throat. 'Just peachy, thanks for asking. I've been kidnapped, forced to drink blood, chased, deflowered, manipulated, laughed at and put on display, and let's not forget spanked and publically humiliated. It's been a top night all around, I think. Oh, I forgot the fainting.' The sarcastic barbs tripped off her tongue, one after the other without pause. 'Yes, absolutely top night. Let's do it again sometime.'

Martinet had to bite his lip in order to hide his smile. She really was quite something. Looking directly at her, a look of bored indifference gracing his features, he replied, 'We're just about to, actually, and I should point out that a lot of the above didn't actually happen. They were nothing more than figments of your imagination. You're still a virgin, darling. Would you like me to prove it to you?' The detached look had gone and his eyes gleamed with a hunger that scared her witless. Her face did not give her away, but her eyelashes fluttered rapidly and her bottom lip trembled.

'The games are about to begin, darling. You'd better buckle your seatbelt up and settle in for the ride.'

A Bedtime Story

There was no time to buckle up. Her whole body floated downwards, to be greeted by the soft crimson satin below. She tried to fight his hold over her, desperately trying to avoid the silky sheets that graced his bed, but her body was no longer under her command. She took a fleeting moment to wonder if it ever would be again.

'Do you want to fight me, princess? Do you want to slam those little fists of yours against my chest and call me names?'

She didn't answer him. Her voice was locked away within her throat once more, at his request. He had obviously heard enough. Her job was to lay there and look pretty, she guessed. *Oh dear God.*

Black ropes slithered up her limbs, coiled around her flesh in a serpentine fashion, winding themselves tighter and tighter, tugging at her limbs. *No.*

'I want you spread wide open for me, Violetta. That way you'll be ready to be taken at a moment's notice. I'll also be able to see how aroused you are for me, and I think you like this body of mine, don't you, Vi?'

Her grunt of protest remained trapped inside her head, but she knew he heard it.

'Oh, I know you find me attractive. Now we're going to work on needs, wants and desires. I'm going to train you to be desperate for the slightest touch my hand may choose to bestow upon your flesh. We're going to make you a hungry, panting, pathetic little slave who lives for nothing more than to pleasure and serve the capricious notions of her master. I've developed quite an active imagination over the years, I'll have you know. We're going to have so much fun together, you and I.'

The words were lost in her head, but they echoed over and over. The rope was reeling her arms and legs tightly into the wooden corners of the four-poster bed and she was beginning to resemble a large 'X' shape. Try as she might, bracing her arms and legs against the firm tugs, did not help in the slightest. Finally she was splayed out to the ropes' satisfaction and the pressure against her wrists and ankles lessoned slightly.

Martinet ran his index and middle finger up and around the small ridge of her ankle. He watched intently as she sucked in air. At this moment in time her mind did not like his fingers upon her. Her body called her a liar though, and trembled at the ridiculously light touch.

His fingers dived under the glistening organza of her gown and crept up a shapely calf. Tiny steps that did little more than tickle her, but she got noticeably more nervous as they tiptoed higher and higher.

'You never thanked me for the arm, you know.'

Violetta told him, in no uncertain terms, just what he could do with his thank you.

'Tsk, tsk. A lady never swears.' He grinned at her, letting the pads of his fingers brush up against the delicate skin of her inner thigh. The nervous pounding of her heart and the flush of heat that turned her cheeks from alabaster to cherry almost instantly, told him all he needed to know. His fingers wandered higher.

'Don't. Stop.' The whispered plea inside her head was frantic.

'Oh, I don't intend to,' he said, deliberately misunderstanding her, and without warning his hand clamped around her sex. She rose into him and gasped. It appeared that her body was once again under her control. Oh who was she kidding? The vamp played her better than Hendrix played the guitar. He knew when to stroke, when to cajole and, more importantly, when to strike.

'My goodness, you're not wearing any panties,' he exclaimed with a devilish gleam in his eyes. 'Why you wanton little...' Martinet didn't finish his last word. Now that Violetta had regained the use of her voice she was about to use it at the top of her lungs. Unfortunately, Martinet was once again one step ahead of her and his face was rapidly descending towards hers. The scream that had been bursting to escape just seconds ago curdled in her throat. Her body pulled against the ropes. Not to get away from him, as it should have, but to move closer. She wanted those talented lips on hers. She wanted his hands on her fevered naked flesh and already, she craved the intense pleasure he could so easily bestow upon her. Covering her lips with his own, he breathed her in. She, on the other hand, couldn't breathe at all. His hands were running up her arms, tracing delicate, rambling patterns on her flesh, while his tongue might have been forked like a dragon's, for it spilled sparkling flames of fire wherever it landed. The ropes rubbed tightly against her wrists and ankles, but she didn't give a damn. She drank him in whole and writhed sinuously underneath his body, begging for more of the same.

'Isn't it hideously embarrassing to be this attracted to your jailor?' His lips left hers with a soft pop and for a moment she just blinked in surprise. Her body was still pulling against her bonds, trying to get ever closer to her talented antagonist. It was horribly humiliating. That alone made her furious.

'Stockholm syndrome's a bitch,' she whispered. 'And isn't it better to do everything you say? If I don't you'll just make me obey, so it makes little difference.' Only her eyes, the true windows to the soul, corrected her statement. They knew differently. And so did he.

'The dress needs to go, darling. I want to see you naked, exposed and vulnerable. It's time to stop thinking and start feeling. I'm going to feed off your body and then I'm going to feed off your emotions. Not only are you fresh blood, but you're fresh entertainment and that's been lacking in my household for some years now.' He gathered the hem of her dress in his two hands and gave an effortless tug. The feeble material had no choice but to split in two, and she was afraid she knew that feeling all too well.

Her head was telling her that this was the worst possible thing that could ever happen to her. Her body was telling her something else entirely. One look at his beautiful face, an angelic face that disguised the heart of a demon, and she was lost. She needed to focus. Distract the bastard. Oh, and while you're at it, get a grip and stop dribbling. He'd tied her to his bed for chrissakes and here she was anticipating the main meal. What the hell was wrong with her? What had he done to her now?

'Is this the only way you can get girls, Martinet? You have to tie 'em up, huh?'

She gave him a look of disgust and rattled the ropes that held her arms for effect. 'You need therapy.'

In response Martinet shredded her lilac dress to bits in one smooth yank of his hands. Tiny pieces of torn fabric shot up in a rush of air and then proceeded to float down slowly, covering the bed in a shimmering confetti of colour. Gently parting the rest of the frothing fabric away from her body, he carefully displayed her breasts and traced a slow path over her concave stomach. 'Not bad, I suppose. Not as beautiful as some, but most certainly not the worst I'll have bedded.' He reached to caress the globe of her right breast, covered in a camisole of fine purple satin that hid nothing. He squeezed the tip of her nipple and laughed when she mewled.

'You didn't answer my question,' she growled in response, turning her face to the side, hoping he didn't examine too closely the stain of heat that was rushing up her chest.

Martinet grabbed hold of his sweater, raised both hands and drew it slowly over his head. He then threw it across the room. Sitting down on the side of the bed he quickly removed his footwear and took off his watch, but Violetta couldn't have said what shoes he wore or repeated whatever words he was now directing at her. She found herself absorbed in the hard planes of his chest, the delicate thatch of hair that covered him in fine swirling patterns and the sharp dip of his hips. When he began to speak at double his original volume, Violetta shook her head as if to clear it of the dark malaise that had fallen over her, but it was of little use. Monsieur Martinet was moving in for the kill. His naked chest was coming towards her at speed and his hands had already tangled in her hair.

'I'll repeat myself for the third time, shall I?' His voice was little more than a whisper against her ear, but she caught the words this time, because he pummelled them into her brain. 'We both know I don't have to tie women up to bed them. For the most part, they throw themselves at me and I take advantage of the fact. This face and body gives me extraordinary privileges that I misuse at every opportunity, to my own advantage. You are not immune to these charms, my dear. The only reason you are tied to my bed is because you'd kill me without a shred of conscience at any given opportunity. Actually, that's not entirely true. I love kinky sex. We can go into detail about that later, though.' His lips twitched. 'Any last requests, darling?' His mouth hovered inches above hers and she knew he was about to begin a war that could only end in death and disaster.

'Please, let me go.' When she moved her lips to talk his were so close that they touched for the briefest instant. She recoiled in shock, trying to bury herself back down into the mattress, but there was nowhere to go.

'Will you promise to stop killing vampires, if I agree to do so?' He enunciated each word carefully and the imprint of his lips, over and over again on hers, made her body ache for something it did not fully recognise.

Violetta's first response was to lie, but he'd bargained on that and the falsehood remained wedged in her throat. No amount of pushing on her part could force it out into the open. So much so, she nearly choked on the single word. Finally giving up, she closed her eyes in defeat and muttered, 'No.'

'You've got a lot to learn around these parts,' he said, using one finger to peel a single eyelid open, giving her no choice but to look at him. He traced a soft path over her eyebrow as he spoke and it should have made her shudder in revulsion, but instead a fierce heat spiralled everywhere. Trying to avoid the hypnotic blue eyes that were trying to bore a path into her head, she eventually discovered it was no use. He held her in place, silently and effortlessly.

'The first lesson is pretty simple. You can never lie to your master.' The finger continued to smooth the hairs over the arch of her brow. His hands were long, beautiful and noticeably cooler than a human's. 'The second lesson is equally clear-cut,' he continued, 'you must obey every order I give you. We both know you'll be testing that one to the limit, but you will learn from your mistakes. There are consequences for every single action you take. You're intelligent. You'll soon figure it out.'

Violetta began to voice one of the million or so questions now buzzing around her head, but it was cut off before a single syllable could be pronounced. His lips and tongue were inside her and she was lost in an inferno of almost painful desire. Her body ignited in all the wrong places. The tips of her nipples pointed and swelled, her lips grew thick and heavy under his onslaught and between her legs there were waterworks of the grandest order. She could feel fluid leaking down her inner thighs and she closed them tightly, mortified.

'That's normal,' came the voice of the beast inside her head. 'It just means that your body wants mine. It's your way of preparing yourself for what's to come.'

Violetta had no idea how he could articulate words, let alone think out a sentence. She was a mess. Her body was whirling at the speed of light, her throat was dry, her heart pounding, and everything was reacting strangely.

'You forget I've done this many times before,' came his inner voice, as his head angled sideways for a deeper kiss. There was a soft scrape of stubble against her cheek and she moaned against him. 'That's it, princess, give yourself up to me. I'll take good care of you.' She didn't believe him. The man was poison and the smallest drop was deadly.

His tongue stroked a sinuous path inside her mouth, and the velvet caress had her body arching for more. His weight pressed into her, dragging her deep into the mattress, but the hard rub of his cock between her thighs was incredible. She felt everything. Every sense was heightened and the smallest touches were amplified to an extraordinary degree. A single finger caressed the underside of her breast, raising a path of goose-bumps in its wake. The satin sheets rubbed against legs as she squirmed underneath him, imparting a single spark of static. Ropes chaffed gently against her wrists, but the tension in her spread-eagled body was so intense it had her gasping. Feeling the strands of his long fine hair as they brushed over her cheek, she moaned heavily as he angled his mouth for another onslaught.

They were the least of her worries. The friction of the hard length of him, rubbing against her naked sex had her almost insane with longing. His hands cupping her breasts and rolling her nipples in his fingers was one of the most amazing sensations she had yet to experience. She could feel a steep mountain of pleasure building inside her body and it desperately wanted to escape; it just couldn't quite work out how.

He finally broke free of her mouth and his voice was a little more ragged around the edges than usual. 'You're such a responsive little thing. I've barely touched you and yet you're nearly creaming the house down already.' Martinet groaned as she moved sharply against him, her hips bucking upward.

As soon as the movement of him grinding against her had stopped and the contact was lost, Violetta's eyes sprang open. She was angry and mostly for reasons she could not fully fathom. There was a few seconds' pause as she gathered up her venom. Then she let it explode. 'What do you mean, barely touched me? You're all over me, you monster!'

'Oh, Violetta, I've barely started with you. I'm still clothed and my tongue has touched nothing more exotic than your beautiful, if somewhat petulant, little mouth. Let's just say it has much grander aspirations. I want to taste all of you and after I've tasted, I intend to feel. What do I want to know? Well, let's see.' He ran his mouth down the curve of her jaw and poured tiny, hot, wet little kisses down the line of her throat. 'How soft you are. How tight you are. Are you responsive to a light touch or a heavy one? Do you like pain, and if so, a little or a lot? These are only some of the things I intend to find out about you, chérie. There is one thing that will become apparent within a very short timescale, though. Whether you will allow yourself to be bent and moulded into a different shape, under my strict tutelage, or whether you will break and shatter. Odds are an even fifty-fifty in my opinion. One moment you appear as delicate and ethereal as a butterfly, but in the next I see the eyes of a killer. I wonder who will win?' He planted a damp kiss where her breastbone dipped, right at the base of her neck.

Violetta couldn't stop herself from squirming under the torrent of kisses he was raining down upon her. He had an unfair advantage in this game. He was able to move. She was but a mere pawn to be played or sacrificed at will. It was a scary thought and one she did not wish to dwell on. 'The killer,' she spat out angrily, as her body rose to meet yet another taste of his feathery lips. The annoying man chuckled in response as his head moved lower, towards the valley of her beasts and, hooking a finger underneath the almost transparent fabric of her camisole, he tugged sharply. The flimsy thing fell apart in his hands and he slid the material to either side of her with a look of penetrating hunger on his face.

'Maybe, but excuse me if I'm not entirely convinced just yet, chérie.' His eyes did not connect with hers as he spoke. They were glued to the twin orbs of pert flesh in front of him. 'You are so very beautiful, far too beautiful to be a deliverer of death, my dear.' His mouth swooped down to suckle at a dusky pink peak and as his tongue laved, and his teeth gently grazed her areola, Violetta nearly shot off the bed, only to have the ropes springboard her straight back down to the mattress.

'You already know that is not the case,' she bit out, somehow, through gasps of tormented pleasure. 'Gilles, Alastair, Rogere, Celeste...' and suddenly she could speak no more. His teeth had clamped around the sensitive point of a nipple and bit, hard. She had to clamp her jaw together to prevent herself from screaming.

'Do not try my patience, chérie,' he said darkly, releasing her now brilliant-red nub from his mouth. 'I have the power to make your life worse than any hell you can imagine. I am systematically going to strip away every shred of your being and rebuild you to my own personal design. You will be the perfect slave. From cooking to cleaning, from satisfying my thirst for blood to my cravings for sex, you will obey me in all matters and you *will watch your tongue*.'

His hand dived under her backside and gripped it fiercely. The scream she had been bottling up erupted from her, and there was no stopping it. His fingernails had buried themselves in one of his earlier raw pink stripes and the pain had her crawling inside herself. There was a slithering sensation all over her lower legs, which had her eyes pouring out of their sockets to find that the rope had turned into twisting black snakes and was unravelling from her ankles in one fluid move. She recoiled and her head spun. Martinet grabbed both her ankles together in one hand and began bending them forward, towards her head. No amount of struggling on her part could stop the motion, and she found her bottom quickly thrust out for his intimate perusal. His spare hand ran over the earlier marks he had made and she squawked in protest.

'Don't like that, hmm? Too bad, because you're going to like this even less.' Straightening out his free hand, so that his fingers were all in line and his thumb tucked away neatly to the side, he raised it behind him... and let it fly. Violetta, in her newly uncomfortable and horribly humiliating position, watched on aghast.

When the smack connected it was not as hard as she had feared, but it still smarted a great deal. Four or five spanks later and she decided she might have to rethink that. He was building the heat up slowly but surely, and her earlier stripes were incredibly sensitive whenever his hand caught them.

'Feel those, do we?' He gave her a look of dark, male satisfaction and smiled as his hand connected with a sharp thwack once again. 'Repeat after me, princess,' he said, giving her a look of piercing disdain, 'I will watch my tongue in my master's presence. You can take as long as you like, but my hand won't stop until I hear those words from you.' As if to indicate he meant business, another heavy smack landed on the seat of her buttocks.

Violetta decided she'd rather swallow crude oil than repeat those words out loud. If he wanted her to call him 'master' he would need to employ stronger tactics, for she would bestow that particular word to no man alive.

'Isn't it awfully lucky that I'm dead then, chérie?' Another hot blow landed on her rump and the heat was building to an intensely uncomfortable level. His blue eyes had a look of utter contempt in them, and she quailed under his gaze. For some reason she had an instinctive urge to obey him, even when every brain cell roared at her to stand her ground.

A few more spanks from his sturdy hands and her body began to shake. 'I will watch my tongue in my master's presence,' he repeated after each slap, as if he were talking to an errant schoolchild. Her backside was blisteringly hot and no amount of struggling could avoid the continuous, ever accurate blows as they imparted more and more fire.

'Stop. Please stop,' she whimpered and her eyes filled with hot, salty tears.

'I will watch my tongue in my master's presence,' was his only reply. His voice was menacing, his displeasure with her increasingly obvious, and the beat of his hand became faster.

She bucked wildly underneath the onslaught, but he held her fast with little effort. Trying to tense the muscles in her ass tightly, to lessen the sting of each strike, she found she was already tiring and it was becoming more and more difficult to fight him. Her mind swirled in a haze of fog-filled pain and escalating arousal. Did vampires need sleep? Did they even get tired? Could he do this all night?

'I can keep this up for two weeks straight, if need be,' came the ominous reply.

She screamed and was annoyed when she couldn't thump her fists around to accompany the sound. Having someone constantly inside your head was infuriating.

'And it's only going to get worse. Now say it, or you'll be getting no sleep tonight and you're certainly not getting any tomorrow.' The speed and intensity increased and he left her speechless for a moment. Knowing every word he spoke was true just made everything worse.

'Stop,' she pleaded. 'Stop. I want to say something.'

He raised an eyebrow, but his hand obligingly stopped in mid-air. 'Speak,' he commanded.

'I will...' a round of coughing ensued, 'watch my tongue...' followed by a choked sob, 'in my...' a giant hiccup ensued where a word was garbled beyond recognition, and then, 'presence.'

Martinet clucked his tongue and chewed his lip. He then pursed his lips and joined his two index fingers together in a sharp point, deep in thought. 'Hmm,' was all he said for several seconds. Then he came at her in a blur of speed and raked his fingernails down the crimson flesh of her buttocks.

'Master. Master, master, master,' she shrieked in response, prepared to do anything to get him off her.

'Give me the whole damn sentence right now or face the consequences.' His gaze had gone from dark to black and his fangs were now visible under the top of his lip. That got her attention as nothing else could. If she was bitten her life was over in so many ways more than one.

'I will watch my tongue in my master's presence.' It was remarkably clear considering her chest had bent back double in order to escape his razor-sharp nails.

He clucked his tongue. 'We have such a long way to go, you and I.' He released her legs and the black ropes crept back around her as if they'd never disappeared, pulling her legs into their former position, her thighs at a forty-five degree angle. But what really had her worried, was that his hands were now on his fly.

'Nooo,' she howled, watching as he slid his black slacks down long legs, heavily corded with muscle.

'You protest too much, darling,' he said lazily. 'Don't fret. You're going to enjoy this.' And those were the last words he said for some time. His mouth was far too busy doing other things to entertain any thoughts of speech. He returned to her breasts and nibbled, sucked, flicked and twisted her nipples around in his mouth. Violetta nearly exploded by those attentions alone, but he knew just when to stop and pull back. He had her sobbing in less time than it took to flick a light switch.

He worked her over with an almost fanatic intensity, caressing wrists, elbows, navels, hips and thighs using his fingertips, teeth and tongue. Every erogenous zone on her body was milked to its maximum potential for pleasure, but stopped short of the magical release she had experienced earlier with him. Her wrists pulled in an almost demented effort at the rope as she tried to rub herself along his body, needing the friction and closeness that remained an elusive few inches away. He had her sobbing in seconds, and the worst part was that his mouth had returned to her throat and was preparing to repeat the entire process all over again. She didn't think she'd survive a second round.

There was a chuckle inside her head at the thought. 'Oh you will. You're much stronger than you think, chérie. I've made some women wait for days before I finally give them what they crave. You might have to wait weeks.' He appeared to have his voice back, because through her pitiful moans and wails of lust and hunger, he began to apprise her of all he had planned. While she could not speak, her tongue thick and useless in a mouth that was almost frothing with desire, he was remarkably eloquent.

'Tomorrow is Sunday,' he murmured. 'We will begin with a late breakfast, followed by a thorough and most intimate bed-bath, and finally we might see about divesting you of your virginity once and for all. It will be the first step in ensuring you are a huntress no more. I am thoroughly looking forward to feeding you, princess. Finding out all your likes and dislikes, and exploiting them where I can.' His lips brushed ever so gently over her sensitised flesh and it was maddening in the extreme. Violetta didn't want to listen to a word that escaped his lips, but nor could she avoid them.

'You will be wholly reliant on me and utterly helpless for the entire week. Feeding, bathing, toileting, care - all this will be in my power to give or withhold, as I see fit. It's going to be an interesting experiment, isn't it? My huntress will now experience what it feels like to be the victim, knowing that nothing but death will await her at every corner. Death and the near, but oh so far, flickering glow of pleasure. Come Monday we'll focus on sucking. We can start on ice-lollipops, before moving on to bigger and better things.' He grinned at her from between the inverted 'V' of her legs before letting his breath tickle her sex. Soft little puffs of air that would do little more than drive her insane. He watched her try to squirm, and to give the girl her dues, she made impressive use of what little leverage she had been given. Twisting this way and that she managed to avoid his teasing technique by working her hips up and down, although it cost her dearly. She had precious little energy left, and as he needed her to conserve it for the next few minutes, he took care of the problem. The steel cuffs floated up from their resting places around the carved rungs of the old oak bed and obediently released their ratchets. Glinting in the beautiful ochre candlelight they danced to attention and waited to do as he bid.

'No, no, no,' she moaned, at a loss as to where to look.

'Are you enjoying your bedtime story, chérie?' The cold steel of the handcuffs pressed at each ankle and wrist and awaited his command. They hovered patiently, and thrash as she might she could not avoid them. His tongue traced a straight line over her sex and he watched her shudder. 'Can you hold still for me, princess? If you can, we might not need the cuffs...'

Martinet knew, without a single doubt, that she would not be able to accomplish the deed. No woman had ever stayed still under his tongue and Miss Cancellaro was not about to be the first. He suckled at her labia, probed her wet entrance with his tongue and palpated her clit with the softest, but most deadly of pointed flicks. Then he attacked. Using every method known in the book he sucked, grazed, slurped, drank and swallowed. The woman was all over the place. He pulled his head up, seeing his reflection in her mind's eye, his features moving strangely in the ambient light as her head swam with sensation. 'The cuffs it is,' he murmured.

There was a sharp click of steel upon steel and then a whir of metal teeth as the handcuffs fastened themselves tightly around every limb. Her eyes burst in shock as she felt their cold pressure and he revelled in the look of fear that marred her features. Rope she thought she could deal with. Unyielding metal was different. It only lasted an instant, and she was quick to recover her wits, but it was gratifying nonetheless.

'You're inside my head,' she said angrily. 'This isn't real.'

He merely smiled in return. There was a shower of incandescent sparks and suddenly a molten line of letters were embedded into each cuff in turn. She shrieked out loud as she saw *Property of M. Martinet* emblazoned on both the upper and lower curves of her restraints. 'It's real enough, pumpkin. You can think of this as the dress rehearsal, in any case. We'll replay the whole thing through properly tomorrow.' He gave her a wink and his tongue descended once more.

This time she could not move more than an inch without hurting herself. The metal held her tightly in its fierce grip and it did not bend. She, on the other hand, would have to bend in all sorts of beautiful contortions before the week was out. Time would tell whether she would be flexible enough to achieve all of his designs, but they could work on perfection. They had all the time in the world.

He felt her blood pressure rise. Violetta's beautiful hips bucked back and forth as he caressed her blushing buttocks and pulled her closer to him. He feasted on her body to his heart's content and watched her blood boil. Thankfully the scent was less potent now he had fed, but she still called to him in a way that most mortals did not. He would have to be careful if he fed from her, but that was a long way off from his plans as of yet. Right now he wanted her on the brink of burning release, but not quite over the edge. Another few sucks and a couple more pointed flicks with his tongue achieved his goal. He ascertained the moment very carefully from within his advantageous hideout inside her head and abruptly pulled away at the moment of climax. She bawled her displeasure around the stone walls of his room, and if he'd had neighbours they would have heard her from about five miles away. Trembling violently, it took her a good few minutes before she gathered up enough energy to address him.

'You told me I'd enjoy it,' Violetta panted. 'Well, I have news for you. You're not quite as good as you think you are.'

The young woman was gloriously furious and she had never looked more beautiful or indeed dangerous as she did at that moment, even tied up as she was. 'Well, you did enjoy it, didn't you? Just not as much as you wanted to. Maybe you should remember not to recite names of your former conquests before we begin getting naked next time. It might help my future generosity in regards to your next orgasm. Or not. No, not, I think.'

He pulled her very own silver dagger from its holster around her thigh and drew the point slowly up her inner thigh, smiling cruelly as she gasped. He then slammed it on the bedside table. 'I give you a week. I'm going to work you over every day for a week, many, many times over, and I'm willing to bet you'd be prepared to use that to end it all in less than seven days' time.' His eyes flew to the dagger, following its carved handle as it gleamed in the candlelight. Hers did the same.

'You're crazy,' she said, her lashes blinking rapidly.

'Seven days.'

'And what if I do?' She looked at him with a mouth wide open in disbelief.

'I'll bring you back to life. For whichever way you turn, this is a game you cannot win. I will have my revenge, one way or another. All that remains to be seen is whether you wish to stay human.'

Violetta shook with helpless fury. The beast had a heart that was blacker than coal, and twice as hard. His last words engraved themselves into her head in vivid relief. They were a stark warning of what was to come. Then the room tunnelled into blackness and she was propelled forcibly into sleep, to await his pleasure on the morn.

Also by C. P. Mandara

Learning the Ropes
Hot to Trot
Named and Shamed
A Rough Ride
and...

Hetty turned her attention back to her subject's face and was quite surprised to see a meek little submissive, almost ashamed of the orgasm she was about to have, panting and heaving for breath whilst nearly foaming at the mouth. Indeed she looked quite tortured in the throes of passion and any Master would be extremely pleased with that particular look during training. Hetty's fingers found their final rhythm and with a measured pressure, they would send the pony girl off to 'O' land in a few seconds...

Meet Jenny. She's rich, spoiled, rude and obnoxious. She's also just been signed up for the BDSM ride of her life - without her consent. An intensive training course at the Albrecht Stables is not what it appears to be and training to become a human pony was not on Jenny's to-do list.

The trouble is, how do you escape when you're tied up, gagged and constantly sexually aroused? Which Master or Mistress do you turn to for rescue? And what do you do if you suspect you might actually be enjoying yourself?

This is Jenny's adventure into the world of BDSM and pony play. She's about to find out just how much effort it takes to become a pony girl and that she has no choice but to excel in every aspect of her training or she may never stand a chance of being released from her bondage.

Book One features Jenny's abrupt induction, where she finds herself being stripped naked, medically examined and intimately measured for her new uniform - as a pony girl.

C. P. Mandara is one of our most popular authors, and her growing list of erotic books are available to download at **www.chimerabooks.co.uk** *now.*

Keep in touch

As mentioned in the intro pages of this book, if you're keen to write erotic fiction and would like our **Author Guidelines**, or you're a published author and have existing work, the rights of which remain with or have reverted to you, we would be delighted to hear from you at **info@chimerabooks.co.uk**.

You can also keep updated on our new releases and special offers at **www.chimerabooks.co.uk**, where you'll also find our complete list of over 300 erotic titles available to download as ebooks.

www.ingramcontent.com/pod-product-compliance
Lightning Source LLC
Chambersburg PA
CBHW070456130626
46555CB00003B/1028